Forsaken
Arbor Falls Book 2

MAYA NICOLE

Copyright 2021 © Maya Nicole
All rights reserved.

No portion of this book may be reproduced in any form without permission from the author, except as permitted by U.S. copyright law.

For permissions contact: mayanicoleauthor@gmail.com

This book is currently available exclusively through Amazon.

The characters and events portrayed in this book are fictitious. Any similarity to real people, living or dead, businesses, or locales are coincidental.

Cover Design by Mayflower Studio

Edited by Karen Sanders Editing
Proofreading by Proofs by Polly

❦ Created with Vellum

AUTHOR'S NOTE

Arbor Falls is a reverse harem romance series. That means the main character will have a happily ever after with three or more men. Recommended for readers 18+ for adult content and language.

This book is dedicated to Silas's motorcycle and the treehouse.

CHAPTER ONE

Xander

*L*aughter filled the night sky as we sat around the campfire, beers in hand, celebrating Liam becoming alpha. It had been a long time coming; for years he had trained under his father, preparing to take over our small pack.

He'd already made a deal with the pack nearby to merge into one. We'd always been on good terms with them, but both of the packs were small and would benefit from combining.

"I'd like to make a toast." I stood and held my beer bottle up to the moon. "All the hard work and sacrifice we've made over the past three years has been worth it to sit here next to our alpha. I'm even more honored to have been chosen as lead beta. My father would have been proud."

I steeled my shoulders, trying to tamp down on the

emotion that threatened to spill over. My father had disappeared a decade ago and we hadn't heard from him since. It nearly killed my mother and left me feeling helpless.

The other betas raised their beers, howled, and then we drank together.

Cal was just handing out another round when a woman's scream came from the trees. We all jumped to attention, our wolves not liking the sound.

"*It's probably just-*" *Austin started, but the woman screamed again.*

I shifted before I could stop myself, taking off into the trees. A woman in our territory was being hurt, and we needed to protect her.

"Alex, stop!" *Liam had already solidified his alpha connection to me, but I didn't heed his command.*

The woman's screams became louder until they cut off abruptly from nearby. I came to a stop and looked around frantically for signs of the woman. The smell of blood in the air overwhelmed my senses. I started in that direction as Liam, Cal, and Austin joined me.

Liam growled, but he must have smelled the blood too, because he didn't say anything. She must have lost half her blood, and from the scent it became clear she was a human, not one of us.

What was a human woman doing in our territory so late at night?

"Jon and his team were supposed to watch the perimeter tonight. I can't get through to him." *Jon was the previous beta who'd retired alongside Liam's father and the rest of his team.*

The sound of dripping hit my ears, and I turned, a howl

leaving me before I could stop myself. Liam couldn't get through to Jon because he and the other two members of his team were hanging from a tree, bleeding out from their throats. Their lifeless, amber eyes stared back at us, warning us to run.

And then something hit my chest.

I woke up panting and clutched my chest to ease the pain. They'd tranquilized us. The last thing I remembered before passing out was them commenting that we were much younger and more suited for what they had in store.

"Hey, man. Are you all right?" The voice was raspy and vaguely familiar.

Where am I? Things had been a bit fuzzy since I woke in the woods after months of being a prisoner. It was like I had been walking through a haze and it was just now lifting enough for me to process what had happened after they took me.

Liam, Austin, and Cal are dead.

My wolf prickled under my skin, threatening to take over, and I pushed him back. I felt like a pup again, trying to gain control of my beast.

Sitting up, I rubbed at my eyes, trying to make sense of what was going on. Metal bars surrounded me. I was in a damn cage again, but this time, I wasn't alone. Cole sat across from me, the concrete floor stained with his blood.

"Did they find us?" Panic rose in my chest, and I jumped to my feet, stumbling a bit from the equilibrium change. I still wasn't used to standing and needed to take things slow.

Cole said nothing, and I looked down at him sitting against the bars of the cage, his hand over his stomach. Blood trickled between his shaking fingers. He was as pale as a ghost, and his jaw was clamped shut so tight he was probably cracking teeth.

"You were shot." The memory came back to me, and I looked around for something to help staunch the bleeding, but nothing was within reach. Hadn't they tended to his wound? Why was he bleeding again?

I went to the door and shook it a few times, the metal rattling but not budging. We were screwed. They had gotten us, and now their sick, twisted games could begin.

"You need to shift and heal. We don't have a lot of time before they come for us again." I knelt next to him and pulled his hand away from his wound. It was still closed, but he had lost a few staples. "How many of them are there?"

"Staples? I don't fucking know, man. Does it matter?" He yanked his hand back and covered his wound. "I can't shift. No energy. Mental and physical." His head lolled to the side before he quickly jerked it up again. "I shouldn't have shifted in the first place, but when they tried to pick me up from outside, I did it to throw them off balance and tried to run."

"How many men are there?" If there were two, we could probably take them if we played it smart. With his condition and my weakness, we'd be at a disadvantage.

"There's three for sure, but probably more." He winced and his eyes shut. "How could I have missed this?"

"Where's Ivy?" I plopped down next to him, and he rested his head on my shoulder. I tensed but didn't pull away. Not too long ago we had been ready to maul each other, but now I felt no ill will toward him.

At least not at that moment.

"I don't know where she is. They knocked Eli out on the lawn, and one of my pack members was getting ready to pick him up to take him somewhere. Two guys were handling me. They punched me in the stomach, and I passed back out. Woke up in here. I'm going to fucking kill Dante."

They didn't find us? Thank fuck for small miracles. A mutiny we could deal with, but if those evil bastards found another pack to torment...

It was quiet for a bit and I assumed Cole had fallen asleep, but he sat forward and looked at me with his brows furrowed. "What's your deal? Who were you talking about that might get us?"

This was not a conversation I wanted to have naked on the floor of a cage. It wasn't a conversation I wanted to have at all.

"It's a dangerous world." I didn't meet his stare and looked out across the room. "My pack had cages like this too. We had cots, though. I didn't appreciate it enough."

"Is that what happened to you?" He wasn't going to stop until I told him, was he?

The memories of the building they kept us in made me shudder. Small cages. The smell of fear. The noises.

"No. My pack..." He wasn't like Eli, who just let me be. I jumped to my feet and tried to open the cage door again. Maybe it had magically unlocked since I'd last tried it. "Eli."

Cole groaned as he repositioned himself. "There's not much we can do for him locked up in here."

"You don't care what happens to your omega?" I glared at him over my shoulder.

"I care, but if I worry about him too much right now, I'm going to lose my mind. When they come back down here, I need one of us not to be crazy." He smirked and then coughed, the sound a bit wet, like he had fluid in his lungs.

"I'm not crazy." At least, I didn't think I was. Okay. Maybe I was a little off kilter, all things considered.

"Could've fooled me." He squinted up at me as if he was having a hard time focusing. "You trespassed into my territory, attacked my omega and my mate. What else could you be?" His head lolled to the side again. He was struggling, and I didn't know what to do to help him.

There was no point in arguing with him. I *had* attacked, but I also hadn't been in control of my wolf. If he needed to focus on my shortcomings to feel better about what had happened to him, I'd let him. For now. "How long do you think we've been down here?"

"Overnight." He lowered himself so he was lying down. "I think I'm dying."

I knelt down beside him and put the back of my

hand against his forehead. "You're burning up. Your wound is probably infected."

He needed food and water to regain his strength so he could shift. We could heal in our human forms, but it was much quicker if we were wolves.

The lock at the top of the stairs unlocked, and the door opened. I stiffened and put myself in front of Cole. He wasn't my alpha or even my friend, but my wolf's instinct was to protect him.

Dirty bare feet came into view first, and then Eli's scent hit me. It was a mixture of fear and anger. He looked like he'd been through hell, with disheveled hair and dirt and dried blood covering his face.

Behind him was a man I didn't recognize, but Cole must have because a guttural noise came from him. "Joseph. Let us out of here right now." He tried to sit up, and I put a hand on his arm to stop him. He needed to stay still and rest.

Eli's eyes filled with tears as he looked past me at Cole. "I need to tend to his wound." He set down a metal bowl with what looked like dry dog food and another bowl that had water outside the cage.

"No, you don't. The alpha was clear that you were to drop off their food and not talk to them. Let's go." The guy completely ignored Cole, keeping his eyes on Eli.

"Eat *all* your food." He winked just as Joseph smacked him on the back of his head and grabbed a fistful of his hair.

"No talking!"

I lunged at the bars, my lip curling back to show my teeth to the man who was practically pulling Eli by the hair back to the stairs. Eli's eyes pleaded with me and he mouthed the word 'eat' before batting the guy's hand away and walking up the stairs in front of him.

"This is all my fault." Cole groaned and pinched the bridge of his nose. "I was so distracted with Ivy that I missed all the signs of a coup."

I shook my head. "Don't blame yourself. It takes longer than a week to stage a coup of this magnitude. He's probably been planning it for a while."

"You sound like you speak from experience."

"No. Just... never mind. Is it all of your betas or just the one?" I found myself wanting to tell Cole everything, but now wasn't the time.

"I think it's just Dante, but I'm not sure. I have five. Well, *had* five."

I reached for the bowl outside of the cage and picked up a few pieces of dog food. It was such a sign of disrespect to feed a wolf that stuff, and I sneered at it. I'd had it before, but that didn't mean I was going to eat it now.

"He said to eat it." I sniffed at it. "It's just dog food."

"He said to eat it *all*." Cole sat up again, and I gave him a look. "It hurts more to lie down."

"Well, if you want some water, you'll have to come to the bars and I'll tip the bowl up for you."

He crawled over, breathing heavily until he could put part of his face between the bars. I lifted the bowl, tipping it so he could drink. When he finished, I did the same. We could use any sustenance we could get. Especially if we were going to make it out of this alive.

Cole reached into the dog food and dug around. "Eli

is smarter than he leads people to believe." He pulled out a small, folded piece of paper and a key. "His words and the wink had purpose."

My fingers itched to rip the note from his hand and read it myself, but I waited patiently as he unfolded it like it was a sheet of tissue paper.

"What does it say?" I asked as his eyes drifted down the page. It didn't look like much was written, but it was taking Cole way too long to read it.

"Fuck if I know. My eyes are blurry." He handed me the paper.

It was written as a list and was fairly sloppy. He'd probably rushed to write it. "They took Ivy. Killed Tyson, Santiago, and Bodhi. Manny and Sara ran. Check surveillance before sneaking out. Don't worry about me."

"Let's go." Cole pushed to his feet and unlocked the cell.

I balled the note in my fist and followed him to the small room that had ten large screens mounted around it with multiple images on each screen.

"We can't leave Eli behind." I owed it to him for taking care of me during my weakest moments. If he hadn't been there, I'm not sure if I would have snapped out of the trance I had been in. "Did you hear me?"

"I heard you." Cole's eyes were glued to one screen, and he clicked a few keys on the keyboard to make one of the four images on the screen larger.

"What is it?" I watched as a group of motorcycles stopped on a gravel road, which I assumed led to the house.

Cole cursed as one of the men stepped forward, gun pointed at another man's chest. They exchanged words, and both men put their guns away and extended their hands. If this was Dante, then we were definitely outnumbered and outgunned.

"Cole?" I needed to know what was going on. He was two shakes of a lamb's tail away from passing out, and I was going to have to take the lead in getting us to safety.

"That's the alpha of the other pack. He must be working with Dante." His fists clenched, and I hoped he didn't decide to start destroying stuff because we needed to be quiet. Plus, he was badly injured. "Let's go."

He brushed past me as the men got back on their motorcycles, turning around and going back the way they came from.

We entered the medical room, and I tensed. How many times had I been strapped down in a room just like this one? I shuddered and shut my eyes.

"Hey." Cole was right in front of me. "I don't know what the fuck you've been through, but right now I need you to take these staples out and bandage me up. Do you think you can do that?"

He shoved an instrument in my hand. My eyes opened, and I blinked rapidly, trying to clear the barrage of images that threatened to overwhelm me. "I think so."

He leaned against one of the tables, and I focused on removing the staples, wincing every time I pulled one out. I wasn't squeamish, but I could almost feel them in my own stomach.

His wound was oozing, and as the last staple fell to the ground, he took a scoop of salve and smeared it over the angry skin. He handed me a roll of gauze and I held it while he turned in a circle.

He grabbed another bandage, and we wrapped that around him before heading to a door leading to a tunnel. Whoever had built the property had really put thought into the finer details.

"I didn't see any men in the den or outside the back doors. That doesn't mean they aren't there or won't smell us." His words were sluggish, and I didn't know how far we were going to make it with the state he was in.

"Should I shift and check it out first?" I didn't particularly want to be back in my wolf form, but I might need to if we wanted to escape.

"No. They'll smell you for sure." His breathing was labored as we climbed the stairs to a door.

We entered the den, which was empty, with the only light coming from an open door across the room from us.

He stopped at a cabinet and pulled out two pairs of shorts, handing me a pair. "If it comes down to it, run. They want me, not you."

"I'm not leaving Eli and Ivy behind." I tilted my head to the side, examining him closely. "Or you."

"We can't help them if we're both locked in a cage. Do you have anyone you can call?" He sat on a folding metal chair and pulled the shorts on. There was no way he was going to be able to run in his condition.

"No." My stomach cramped at the thought of my pack. Gone. All of them.

And now, I might lose my new pack.

"The next nearest pack is two hundred miles to the southeast. In the Tahoe area. They should be able to help." He pushed to his feet and put a hand on my shoulder. "Thank you."

What was he thanking me for, and why was he talking like he wasn't going to make it?

The door we had just come through burst open and Cole met my wide eyes. I nodded, and we both bolted for the back door.

My hand was on the doorknob when something hit my back, delivering a pinch of pain. Numbness spread from the area and I fell to my knees, the tranquilizer rendering me helpless.

Fuck. We weren't going to make it.

CHAPTER TWO

Ivy

*C*old. I was trapped inside an ice cube, frozen solid and unable to breathe. I pushed and pushed at the solid walls of ice surrounding me, trying to break free. My entire body was both numb and on fire, like a million fire ants were biting my flesh, spreading their venom.

A figure appeared on the other side of the ice, not completely visible through the opaqueness. His dark shadow terrified me but excited my wolf.

My wolf.

She was fading, slinking back into the darkness, pawing to escape. I reached for her, but her paws slipped through my hands.

Clink. Clink. Clink.

The man was chiseling his way to me, but the cold was too much.

"Bunny."

I woke with a pounding heart, sitting straight up and looking for the sound of the voice. I was alone, naked in a bedroom that wasn't mine. A deep chill ran through my body, pulling a whimper from my cracked lips.

I pulled up the thick blanket that was over me to cover my chest and tried to come to terms with what had happened. I didn't remember much, but what I remembered made my blood turn to ice.

Or was that just the fact that Dante had thrown me into the icy river with water that was freezing from the melted snow runoff from the mountains?

I should have been dead. No one survives that long in cold water. I'd barely breathed with the muzzle keeping my mouth closed and the water often covering my head.

Taking a deep breath to calm myself, the masculine scent that infiltrated my nose was overwhelming.

Mate.

Whiskey and a faint hint of pine made my wolf stir from the corners of my mind. I thought I'd lost her. Was that even possible?

Silas.

I don't know how I knew the scent was him, but I did. Why was I in his room, and was I in danger? My wolf didn't like the idea of him being an enemy and curled back up, my body feeling the need to burrow in the bed.

Instead, I forced myself to stand, wrapping the thick blanket that had a giant wolf head printed on it around me. Oh, God. Yet another man had seen me naked. It was the norm, I knew that now, but it still irked me.

I shuffled across the room to the door, which was solid metal like the rest of the room, with a single skylight in the ceiling. It felt like I was in some kind of industrial building.

The door was locked from the inside, and I put my ear against it, the metal sending a chill through me. There were faint sounds of voices, both male and female, coming from the other side, but they were distant.

I needed a weapon. I wanted to believe that I was safe, but I had thought I was safe at Cole's and was wrong. Were Cole, Eli, and Xander okay?

Checking the normal hiding spots—under the mattress and in the nightstand—I came up empty-handed. I shivered and continued to the dresser, which had clothes hanging out of drawers and scattered nearby on the floor. He wasn't the tidiest of men.

I pulled a shirt from a drawer and sniffed it, making sure it was clean, and found a pair of sweatpants that had seen better days.

It had to be well into the afternoon, judging from the light coming through the skylight. How long had I been passed out since I was found?

The bathroom was small, but had all the necessities. I locked the door behind me and turned on the water, hoping it was hot because I still felt like I'd been swimming in an ice bath for days.

I should be freaking out more. Hell, I had done nothing except try to escape since turning twenty-six. I wanted a do over.

I stepped under the warm spray and my skin burned as the water hit it. I sighed in relief as the chill began leaving my body. If drowning didn't kill me, the chill should have.

Not wanting to stay in a vulnerable state for long, I quickly washed my hair and body before climbing out and cursing that I hadn't looked for a clean towel. Instead, I used the blanket to dry off, although that probably wasn't much better than the towel on the rack.

After pulling on the clean clothes, I listened at the door, and then went back into the room.

What the hell am I going to do?

I needed to find out what was on the other side of the door. If I opened it a crack, I could assess the situation and then plan my escape and find a damn phone.

I looked down at my bare feet before going back to the dresser to grab a rolled-up pair of socks. A picture behind a pile of t-shirts on top of the dresser caught my eye, and I picked it up to examine it.

Three men stood with their arms around each other's shoulders, two toddlers sitting on the ground in front of them. My heart sped up, realizing what I was looking at.

Cole and Silas both looked similar to two of the men, but the man in the middle... a chill ran down my spine as I brought the picture closer to my face. It was an old photo that was creased and a little faded.

They were laughing, the man in the middle with his head thrown back slightly. How had no one seen the similarities? Maybe it had been so long ago, and they'd never seen *me* laugh like that. There weren't any other pictures for me to see, but something about it felt right.

I flipped the picture over and took the photo out of the frame, folding it carefully and putting it in my pocket. I'd need to stare at it a little longer to be sure.

Not to be deterred from my escape, I spotted a pair of boots shoved under the edge of the bed and put them on. They were too big, but they would have to do.

I listened at the door again. It was silent on the other side, so I unlocked it as quietly as possible and cracked it open to peek out.

The room I was in was upstairs with a large open area below. It had windows lining almost the entire upper portion of the metal walls. It was a warehouse or factory of some kind.

I sniffed the air, giving my wolf senses a shot to warn me of anything, but all I smelled was other wolves and food. I'd quickly come to realize that wolves smelled like freshly turned dirt with subtle differences between each wolf. An easily identifiable smell among the aroma of hamburgers and french fries. My stomach rumbled at the idea of biting into a juicy burger covered in gooey cheese. *Not now.*

I lowered to my hands and knees and crawled out the door onto the metal platform that overlooked the entire space. Staying low to the ground might be my best bet of getting out undetected.

I could see much more of the space once I was out

of the bedroom. Quite a few people—wolves—lived or spent a lot of their time there. There appeared to be rooms on the other side of the space, and in the middle was a large lounge area, a dining area, and a swinging door that looked like it led into a kitchen.

On one wall was a large mural of wolves howling at the moon with *West Arbor Pack* written underneath. It was a powerful image, and had I not been in dire circumstances, I would have stared at it longer. Wolves sure did like their spray-painted art.

Rising to my feet but staying hunched down, I crept down the metal stairs, flinching every time my foot made a sound as I stepped.

Once at the bottom, I darted behind a group of chairs in a corner. It didn't provide the best cover, but was better than being out in the open while getting a lay of the land.

Where was the door? The space was so large with so many doors that I wasn't sure I'd ever find the exit.

Taking a deep breath, I decided on a door directly across from the large mural. If it were my place, I'd want the mural to be the first thing someone saw coming in. It was a straight shot across the lounge area, but I was going to stay close to the perimeter of the room and hope for the best. I hadn't seen anyone yet, but I'd heard them earlier.

About halfway to the door, it slammed open, and a scary-looking old man walked in. I came to a halt as our eyes met. His widened, and I made a split-second decision to go for the nearest door.

"Stop!" The man's voice cut off as I slammed the

door and turned the lock behind me. His fists pounded on the door as I leaned against it.

He shouted, and then other voices joined him. Shit. I needed to think fast.

I was in a storage room that had boxes stacked practically to the ceiling. There was a window on the far side of the room, and that was my only shot at getting out. The banging on the door had stopped, and it was only a matter of time before the man found the key or got the door open.

The window was high up, but there was a desk underneath that would give me just enough boost to pull myself up. I hadn't done pullups in a while and was still feeling the effects of what Dante had done, but there was no other choice.

Passing the towers of unmarked boxes, I wondered what was inside them, but my curiosity would have to do without the satisfaction of finding out. I climbed onto the desk, lifted the wooden dowel wedged in the track, and slid the window open.

Hooking my arms around the windowsill, I grunted in an unladylike way as I hauled myself up. It was a tight squeeze, and I was left with no other choice but to fall headfirst.

Somehow, I landed on my hands and knees, the sting of the fall quickly fading. It had to be a wolf thing.

It was midday, and the sun felt glorious against my face as I tilted it toward the sky. There was no time to enjoy it though because I heard yelling from around the corner.

Without knowing where the hell I was going, my

feet took me away from the voices to the corner of the building. It was surrounded on three sides by forest, but to one side was a large gravel parking lot, and on the other side of that was a highway.

Not wasting any time, I darted across the parking lot and was out the gate before I braved a glance back. A few women and men had just come out of the front door and one pointed at me.

I started walking as fast as I could down the side of the highway, cars zooming past in a blur. I had never hitchhiked before and didn't know if it even worked, but it was my only chance.

They didn't seem to be chasing me, though. There were enough cars passing on the highway that seeing a woman running from a pack of people would warrant a nine-one-one call, and I doubted they wanted that.

I slowed to a brisk walk and put my thumb out, hoping someone would take pity. My appearance wasn't too horrible, although my clothes were baggy, and the boots looked like clown shoes.

A few minutes into my hike, a Highway Patrol car pulled off to the shoulder. It was the best luck in the world, or the worst. I didn't have identification or even a phone.

As I approached the car, the officer got out and pushed his aviators onto the top of his head. "Everything okay, ma'am?"

"Yeah, my boyfriend kicked me out of the car. Well, ex-boyfriend." It seemed completely plausible and would explain why I had nothing with me. "Can I get a ride into Arbor Falls?"

I had no clue where the hell I was, but if I was in Silas's territory, I couldn't be that far from town.

He looked me up and down. "Did he hurt you?"

"Just my pride." I laughed and then stopped when the officer's frown deepened. "I'm fine. Just... need a ride since I don't have my phone. I live in Arbor Falls."

He assessed me for another few moments and then lowered his glasses back over his eyes. "Climb on in." If he hadn't pulled over, I might have been walking for a while.

Once my seatbelt was on, he pulled back onto the highway and turned in the opposite direction of the way I was walking. That would have been a fun walk going nowhere.

"I can take you to the clinic or the shelter if you need an exam or a safe place." He didn't take his eyes off the road as we wound our way along the highway.

"Really, I'm fine. We just got in a bad argument, and he broke it off." I gave him my address, and we rode the rest of the way in silence.

Before I got out of the car, he handed me his business card. "If you change your mind, please don't hesitate to call."

I appreciated his concern, even though it was unwarranted. "Thank you."

He waited until I was safely inside my house—thank God for hidden keys—before he pulled away. I leaned back against the door and let out a shaky breath, holding in the tears that threatened to fall.

I was home.

I PACED MY BEDROOM, keeping an eye on the window that looked out to the front. I had changed into an old pair of jeans and a sweater I hadn't packed and was considering my options.

A small part of me wanted to jump in my car and head for the hills. I had friends who could protect me, but that would mean revealing myself to more than just Riley, and I wasn't sure that was a wise idea.

The other part of me wanted to go show Dante who he'd fucked with. The anger I felt toward him was threatening to bubble over, and my wolf's sole focus was on ripping his throat out. He'd caught me off guard, and I wouldn't let that happen again.

I rubbed my chest and took surveillance of the front again. I needed to save my mates.

A crazed laugh bubbled out of me, and the next thing I knew I was full on sobbing. I didn't sign up to almost die twice in just a week or to have three... no... four mates.

Grabbing some tissue off the nightstand, I blew my nose and wiped my tears. I needed to be strong. If not for myself, then for the three men who might be hurt or worse. If Dante was willing to throw a bound woman in the river, what else was he capable of?

I'd go to Cole's, fight Dante, and take back what was mine. There was no other choice. My wolf rose up inside me, and for once, I didn't push her back. We'd do this together.

CHAPTER THREE

Silas

*P*ulling into the lot outside the den, I finally let my shoulders relax. Cole was being taken care of for the time being, and all I could think about was getting back to my mate.

I'd been ready for an epic throwdown that was a long time coming, but then Dante had stopped my envoy not far from the main house and den.

"Silas, what brings you to my territory?" Dante stood in the middle of the gravel road, his arms folded across his chest.

I didn't know him well, just from word of mouth from my betas. They said he was a hard ass and a traditionalist, something Cole was not. I'd heard Cole had let the true omega's twin take her place. That was unheard of and even more reason to make my move. He was making bad decisions and had nearly killed my bunny.

"I'm here to speak with your alpha." *I got off my bike because he wasn't moving, and I'd probably have to put him on his back. He was about the same size as me, but I knew I was the stronger wolf.*

I should have done this a long time ago, but there had still been a tiny part of me that hoped Cole's father would admit to killing Baron and we'd reconcile. That didn't seem like it was going to happen, so I had to stand my ground in the name of my father.

Bone and Rover got off their bikes and cracked their knuckles in warning as I stepped closer.

"Ah, my alpha?" *He laughed.* "Cole is no longer the alpha, I am."

I bit the inside of my cheek to keep myself from reacting. "Excuse me? Since when?"

"Since yesterday. I have a lot to take care of, so if you and your men don't mind, we can arrange a meeting for next week to discuss reconciling our differences." *He reached behind him, and when his hand fell back to his side, he had a gun.*

I quickly drew mine, pointing it at Dante's chest. He did the same, and my betas stepped forward, but I told them to stand back using our connection.

"Is Cole dead?" *As much as I hated him, my heart stuttered to a stop as I waited for an answer.*

"No, but he's being taken care of." *Dante cocked his head to the side.* "Why are you here?"

I narrowed my eyes. "He hurt something of mine."

"I see." *He rubbed his jaw with his free hand and seemed*

to think a little too hard about what to say. "If he's still alive in a week, we can discuss you taking a stab at him."

I didn't like the vibes this guy was sending off, and I stepped forward, staring him down. There was no doubt in my mind that if I challenged him right here and now he'd fail... except putting guns in the equation might change things a bit.

He lowered his gun and stuck out his hand. I looked at his outstretched hand for a moment before lowering my gun and taking it, squeezing hard enough to break human bones. We weren't human, though.

"I'll be seeing you again, Dante."

I walked back to my bike and got on, my betas following my lead.

I FOLLOWED my betas and enforcers inside the den. Most of my men were working their nine to fives, so I'd gone with the gun half-cocked. I desperately needed to work on my impulsivity because if Dante had been trigger happy, someone could have been injured.

Cole would get what was coming to him in due time.

"Alpha," Carly purred, putting herself in my face as soon as I was in the door. Her hand slid up my chest and wound around to the back of my neck. "I'm so glad you're okay."

I took hold of her hand and removed it, eliciting a whine from her. "I told you, Carl, no more."

That conversation a few days ago had gone really well. She didn't know I had a mate, but I told her there was someone else. She was never someone serious anyway, just a warm body.

"Boss, the woman ran," Ray said from across the room. "We tried to chase after her, but she was gone by the time we got out onto the highway."

I shut my eyes and my chest heaved as anger swelled inside me. "What do you mean she's gone?"

They were a bunch of fucking idiots. No wonder I kept losing pack members to other packs.

"Uh... she ran. We couldn't catch her. She went out through a window in the storage room." He shrugged like he hadn't just lost the most important person in my life.

"Why the fuck was the door to the storage room unlocked?" I marched over to it and threw it open. "Still unlocked! Jesus Christ! I swear, it's a miracle we haven't been robbed! Get off your ass and fix it before I fix you."

I stormed back out of the building, slamming the door behind me. Bone and Rover were hot on my heels.

"Boss, what do you want us to do?"

"Fucking stay here and call me if she comes back." I knew where she might have gone, and she certainly wouldn't be coming back on her own. "And lock that damn door and secure the window."

Fifteen minutes later, I turned down Ivy's street, hoping I was right and she'd gone home. She wouldn't go back to the East Arbor Pack, not after what they did to her.

Just as I turned into her driveway, the garage door

opened, and a vehicle started. Her eyes met mine in the rearview mirror and they narrowed. The reverse lights turned on and I barely had enough time to dive off my bike before she was backing into it.

"What the fuck?" I yelled, jumping to my feet and rounding the car to the driver's side door. "What are you doing?"

She revved the engine and attempted to back up over my bike that was now right behind her car. She was insane.

The back tires of the car made it over my bike, and then the car stalled and made a horrible screeching sound. She pounded her fists on the steering wheel and then threw the car in park and turned it off.

I took my helmet off and ran my fingers through my hair, trying to tell myself it was just a bike and it was probably fine. Maybe a scratch or two, a broken side mirror, a popped tire. It would be fine.

A giant kitchen knife appeared in her hand as she stared at me through the window. Her chest heaved, and her face was almost as red as her hair. It would have been sexy if I wasn't the reason for her wrath.

The door flew open and she jumped out, holding the knife in front of her. I dropped my helmet and held my hands up in surrender. "Look-"

"You look. You're going to give me your cell phone and then sit down and wait for the cops to get here." She was shaking so badly that I probably could have taken the knife from her if I went at her from the right angle.

"We do not need cops involved with this, bunny. Put

the knife down and we can go inside and talk." I took a step forward, and she took a step back, right against the front end of the car, halting her retreat. "I'm not going to hurt you."

"I don't believe you." She adjusted her grip, seeming unsure about how to hold the knife to stab me if I got closer. "Why was I naked in your room?"

"You know why, bunny." Another step. "You don't need to worry now, though. Dante took care of Cole so he can never hurt you again."

"Wh-what?" The knife fell to the ground, and before she could try to grab it again, I kicked it under the vehicle. "Cole didn't hurt me! But *you* did!"

She smacked me across the face, and I covered the sting with my hand. "Jesus, what was that for? I didn't hurt you!"

"You made us crash!" She kicked out, and I turned before her foot could connect with my balls. "I was perfectly fine until then! This is all your fault!"

Her shrieking was going to attract attention. I grabbed her around the waist and covered her mouth with my hand, practically dragging her back into her open garage with her heels, trying to gain traction on the cement. It was a stupid idea, because I was sure she'd hate me even more for it, but she was a feisty one and she left me with no other choice.

I uncovered her mouth to press the garage door button, and she screamed bloody murder. It was a piercing scream that made my ears hurt and my blood pressure shoot sky high.

"Enough!" My alpha voice came out next to her ear,

and her scream cut off abruptly as the door descended, leaving us in the dark. "I'm not going to hurt you."

"Please... just let me go save my mates." Her voice was muddled, and she sniffled.

Ah, shit. Was she crying? And what the hell did she mean by *mates*?

"You're shaking like a leaf. Let's get you inside and you can yell and hit me some more, okay?" When she didn't respond, I loosened my hold. "The crash was an accident, by the way. My idiot betas took it a little too far."

Her breaths came in gasps, and I spun her around in my arms, pulling her against my chest. She tried shoving me away but then sank against me like all the fight had left her.

"That's a good bunny." I smoothed my hand over her hair several times before scooping her up like she was my bride and opening the door. "Tsk. Why don't you lock the door? Don't you watch Dateline?"

"Stop calling me bunny." She had her face buried against my shoulder, and instead of putting her down on her own two feet, I sat down on her couch, keeping her pulled close.

"We're mates." I buried my fingers in her hair and lowered my nose to it, breathing it in. "You used my shampoo."

She pulled back and gave me a death stare. My nuts instantly pulled closer to my body to protect themselves. She'd rip them off and shove them down my throat if I pissed her off, I was sure of it.

"We need to go get them. Dante needs to be

stopped." She'd completely ignored my declaration that she was my mate. Did she not feel the pull toward me? The overwhelming need to just be close?

I was confused why she wanted to stop Dante, and I brushed the hair out of her face. "I went to kick Cole's ass in your name and Dante told me he had Cole handled."

She wiggled out of my arms and stood, staring down at me. "You think Cole hurt me? Cole is my mate! So are Eli and Xander!" She threw her hands in the air before letting them fall with a smack against her jean clad thighs. "And now apparently you."

She rounded the coffee table and paced in front of it. I sat back, propping an ankle on a knee, and watched as her long legs took her from one end of the room to the other. She had a strong stride for just being found half-dead in a river.

"If Cole didn't hurt you, then who did?" I crossed my arms.

"Dante."

"So Cole didn't tie you up and toss you in the river?"

Stopping abruptly, she glared at me. "I see why you and Cole don't get along."

"What's that supposed to mean?" My boot hit the ground, and I leaned forward with my forearms on my knees.

"It means you're an idiot. Dante threw me in the river. He shot Cole, waited for the perfect time, then tranquilized me. I'm going to kill him."

I jumped to my feet, definitely feeling like an idiot. She was making my thoughts unclear. I usually wasn't so dense, but apparently with her I couldn't think logically. It made so much sense now! That son of a bitch. I was going to rip his head off and shove it so far up his ass he would need a plunger to get it out.

A loud knock on the door interrupted my inner tirade, and our eyes met. I was closer and looked out the peephole. "Damn it, it's a cop," I whispered.

"Well, you dragged me screaming into my garage. Sit down on the couch and act casual." She wiped her tears and smoothed her hair.

Fuck. Was she going to have me arrested? It wouldn't be the first time, but being locked up right then was not in the plans. I did as she asked and propped my feet up on the table, crossing my ankles.

She opened the door with a smile on her face. "Officer, what can I do for you?"

His eyes immediately fell on me and his hand settled on top of his holster. "Ma'am we had a few calls about screaming. I noticed the car out front has hit a motorcycle in the driveway. Do you need help?"

Ivy stood a little taller. "Do you arrest cheaters? This fucker was cheating on me with his best friend, so I ran over his bike. I was screaming because I found out about his cheating by testing positive for an STI. Can you believe that bullshit?"

I bit my inner cheek and schooled my expression. She was good, a little too good.

"Ah, well." His hand lifted from his holster to his jaw, and he looked around her at me. "Sir, do you want to press charges for the bike?"

Standing, I ran both my hands through my hair.

"No, Officer. We didn't mean to disturb the neighbors. Just a little foreplay before I beg for forgiveness on my knees."

He turned a little red in the face. "All right, you folks, have a nice evening. Maybe look into some couple's counseling. A storm is supposed to roll in tonight. Might want to get this mess out here taken care of before we're buried in snow again." With one final glance into the house, he retreated down the porch steps.

"Thank you, officer." She shut the door and put her forehead against it. "We need to go now."

I chose my words carefully. "If we go now, we go in unprepared, not knowing how many men we're up against. We have to play this smart."

"The longer we wait..."

I put my hand on her shoulder and turned her around. "I promise you, Dante will pay for what he's done to you... and the others." I gritted my teeth. "He won't know what hit him."

CHAPTER FOUR

Ivy

*E*ven I had to admit I'd gone a little crazy when I tried to run over Silas. I'd opened the garage door and there he was, all six feet of him in ripped jeans, a leather jacket, and his blue eyes staring back at me.

Something had come over me. The need to punish him for nearly killing Cole and me on my birthday and setting off the whole shit storm of a life I was now leading.

And it had only been a week.

I was at war with myself. I wanted to believe the motorcycle god blocking my exit was there to help me, but what if it was a ploy to take over the East Arbor Pack?

I did what any red-blooded, sleep-deprived, almost

killed two times in a week female would do and I flipped out. He dove from his bike and I backed over it, getting stuck.

It would have been hilarious if I hadn't felt like I was the one on the losing end. My life was completely flipped upside down and I had enough unanswered questions to annoy even a preschool teacher.

"What are you thinking about?" Silas was driving my car back to his den, which he had convinced me was the safest place for us. Dante wanted me dead for whatever reason, and if he found out I was at home, he'd probably come after me.

"Just about how good it felt to destroy something." His bike wasn't destroyed, but it needed some serious repairs before he could ride it again.

Was I sorry I did it? No.

He had looked like he was going to cry when a few of his guys showed up to get my car off it. Luckily, my car was fine. He insisted on driving us because he said I didn't know how to drive. I couldn't blame him.

"One of the pack members has a motorcycle repair shop, so you're lucky." He was driving with one hand on the wheel and the other on the headrest of my seat. I could almost feel him touching my hair, even though he wasn't.

From the moment Silas touched me, I came alive inside and wanted more in whatever way possible. I didn't understand why I had four mates, or if there might be more, but they made me feel invincible.

Four cocks were going to be enough to handle, and I hadn't even been on a date with any of them yet. I wanted Silas so badly, but also didn't know if acting on my urges would be considered cheating.

"When do you think we're going to make our move?" Twisting my hands in my lap, I focused on the scenery outside. My wolf was impatient and wanted to take back what was ours. "The longer we wait, the more time he has to sink his claws in."

"With the storm rolling in... probably not for a few days." He took my hand, bringing it to rest with his on the center console. I let him because it soothed my wolf. The initial freak out of being a wolf was long gone, and now I couldn't imagine her not being there.

"Wouldn't during a storm be the best time? They won't expect it and it will mask our scents, right?"

"It's risky. Forecast says blizzard-like conditions with up to two feet of snow." His thumb rubbed across my hand, and I shut my eyes. "Late season storms are always the worst."

"I wish I knew phone numbers to contact pack members, but I hardly know anyone." I opened my eyes and looked at his large hand covering mine. "Maybe if we could contact some people, we could get a feel for whose side they're on."

He grunted and turned off the highway into the lot for the building I escaped from. It looked like any run-of-the-mill warehouses on the outside and didn't appear to have any neighbors.

"The only person I communicated with was Cole. Through email because he never let me get in a word if we spoke."

I found that hard to believe but didn't say otherwise. He was showing me his cards, and it was clear he didn't really want to save anyone.

"How many members do you have in your pack?"

"I don't know. A hundred or so." He parked my car and shut it off. "We're a smaller pack, but that means we all know each other and get along like family."

"Then you should know the exact number of pack members you have." Unhooking my belt, I turned toward him. "Cole used to be your family. He knows exactly how many pack members he has."

He stiffened and squeezed the steering wheel. "That was a long time ago, and of course he knows how many. He gets that information from his omega. Don't let him fool you into thinking otherwise." He opened the door and got out before I could respond.

The issues between the packs ran deep, and I inwardly groaned. Of course I'd have a mate in each of the packs. Things just couldn't be easy.

Taking a deep breath, I got out of the car and followed him to the front door. My keys were in his jacket pocket, and I needed to keep an eye on him to see if he put them somewhere.

The picture I'd taken from his room was burning a hole in my pocket. But when would be the right time to ask him who the other man was?

We entered the building and Silas came to a stop, running his fingers through his hair. "I apologize in advance for anything idiotic my pack members say to you."

"Alpha!" One of the guys who I had first seen during

my escape jumped up from the video game he was playing. "You found her."

"No thanks to you." Silas put his hand on the small of my back and led me into the kitchen through a swinging door. "Carly. This is Ivy. She'll be staying with us for a while. Make sure she's fed while I go take care of the idiots."

I opened my mouth to protest about staying awhile and about him leaving me alone with a female who narrowed her eyes as soon as Silas turned his back.

"Where'd he find you? Hounder?" It took me a second to process what she said, and I snorted. This chick was jealous.

"Nope." Since she hadn't moved, and I didn't trust her not to spit in whatever she fed me, I went to the large industrial refrigerator and opened it. It was jam packed with food. How many people did they feed there?

"Silas and I are a thing." She was hovering behind me now, closer than I would have liked.

I pulled out some turkey, cheese, and mayonnaise and turned to face her. "Is that so?"

"I heard you aren't even a normal wolf. That you're red." Maybe if I ignored her, she'd go away. She had barely even met me and she was already starting shit. "No wonder the other pack threw you away like trash."

What did she just say?

Dropping the food on the metal counter, I turned around and grabbed her by the front of her shirt. Her eyes widened in shock and my voice took on an authoritative quality as my wolf took over. "The only trash in this room right now is you. So, I suggest you deal with my presence or find somewhere else to be. Am I clear?"

She whimpered and looked down. "S-s-sorry. It won't happen again."

I let her go and her shoulders sagged, in defeat or relief, I wasn't sure. Clearing my throat, I turned back to my food, not sure what the hell had just happened. "Where's the bread?"

It was like my wolf had taken over my entire being, or was that me? I'd always stood up to bullies, but never gotten in their face or touched them. Thinking back on it, maybe I should have.

Opening the mayonnaise, I looked over my shoulder. "Bread? Knife?" Carly gaped at me. "What now?"

"You're an alpha." Her brows furrowed. "But how? What pack?"

I threw my head back and laughed. "I'm not. Trust me. I'm just a woman who wants a sandwich before I get hangry. You don't want me to get hangry, do you?"

Carly blinked at me in disbelief for another few seconds before turning to a cabinet and pulling out two different kinds of bread and getting a butter knife from a drawer. "I felt it. We can sense these things, especially when a higher-ranking wolf talks to us like you just talked to me."

I picked the marbled rye and began making a sandwich. The last thing I wanted to worry about was the idea of being an alpha. I barely understood what it meant to be a wolf.

"Look, I don't know what you think you felt, but I

barely even shifted for the first time a week ago." I made a sandwich and put everything away. "Maybe that's why Dante threw me in the river."

She leaned against the opposite counter and studied me. I didn't know whether to be nervous or intrigued by her sudden change of heart.

"Dante's the one who did that to you?" She shuddered. "I uh... matched with him on Hounder a few years back before he became a beta."

I really needed to check out this Hounder to see what it was all about. Was it supposed to be the wolf version of Tinder? I snorted and took a bite of my sandwich.

"Couldn't get it up? Or wait... I bet he's a two-pump chump." This woman had just insulted me not more than five minutes prior, and there I was talking shit with her.

"I didn't let him touch me. He just talked about himself like he was God's gift to the wolf world. I'm not surprised he went after Cole. You could have stopped him I bet." She opened another cabinet and waved her hand in front of it like a game show model. "We have a lot of chips if you would like some."

"It's almost dinner time, isn't it?" I finished the last bite of sandwich. I had been so hungry I'd practically inhaled it.

She sighed. "Yes, but it's Bone's turn to cook, and he takes forever."

"Bone? Someone's nickname is Bone?" I shook my head in disbelief. "What's your nickname?"

She looked at her nails. "Carl."

I snorted a laugh, and she joined in. "Better than bunny."

"Bunny is an excellent name." Silas sauntered back into the kitchen looking like a tall glass of whiskey that I wanted to drink. "You ladies getting along?" He gave Carly a stern look.

I didn't know what was going on between them, but I held onto the edge of the counter, resisting the urge to go over to him and stake my claim in front of Carly. I needed to get out of there before I made a bad decision.

"I'd like to lie down for a bit before dinner. When did you find me, anyway?" I wasn't tired, but being away from them might help me regain some clarity.

"This morning." Silas's eyes fell to where I was still gripping the counter, my knuckles turning white. "It's pretty amazing you're already recovered, actually."

I let go of the counter and shoved my hands in my pockets. "Where can I take a nap?"

He came around the counter and guided me by the small of my back. Everyone watched us as he led me up the metal stairs to the room I'd been in earlier. "Did Carly give you a hard time?"

"I put her in her place." I was sure he'd hear about it from her. "Is she okay with me sleeping in your bed? Will you be sleeping in hers tonight?"

He shut the door behind us and turned to me, a smirk forming. He ran his hand down his short beard. "Bunny, are you jealous?"

Ignoring his question, because shit, I was jealous, I sat on the edge of the bed. "Okay. What's with the bunny nickname?" I ogled him taking off his leather jacket and throwing it on the bed next to me.

"Answer my question first." He leaned against the door, crossing his arms over his chest. His white t-shirt pulled deliciously against his biceps and his pecs.

"I hardly know you. You could be working with Dante for all I know."

He pushed off the door and fell to his knees in front of me. He moved so fast I jumped and scooted back as he looked at me with the sincerest of eyes. "I would never hurt you."

Taking my hands, I felt like I was the center of his universe. But how? We barely knew each other, and if he was with another woman, I didn't want to be a home-wrecker, even if he was part of my harem of mates.

I laughed at myself and his face clouded in concern. Random laughing did appear a bit crazy. "She said you were together." I pulled my hands from his. "And I'm with Cole and Eli. It wouldn't be fair to them if we just..."

"Just what, bunny?" He braced his hands on either side of the bed. "Cole and Eli couldn't protect you."

I growled, my wolf rising. He fell back on his ass and stared up at me, his blue eyes dilating and then flickering to amber. It should have been concerning to see his wolf's eyes staring back at me, but I was oddly satisfied she'd shaken him up a bit.

I stood up and glared down at him. "The correct response should have been, *I completely understand, Ivy.*"

"Who the fuck *are* you?" His voice was harsh as he

climbed to his feet and stepped toward me. I didn't move an inch.

Keep your cool. He won't hurt you. Maybe.

I reached into my pocket and pulled out the folded photo I'd snagged earlier. I held it up to his face, and he snatched it from me and then looked over at his dresser. "You took my photo? Why?"

"Who's that man in the middle?" I crossed my arms to make sure he didn't come any closer.

He took my stance as a hint and backed up. "Baron Arnold, the previous alpha before Cole's father killed him." He walked to the dresser and put the photo in a drawer. "He was like a second father to me."

"I think he's my father."

∼

THE PERFECT WAY TO get Silas to shut up and give me space was to drop a bomb of information on him. He stared at me for at least two minutes, and then, without another word, left the room.

Carly had come in sometime later and told me it was time to eat, and I mumbled that I wasn't hungry. And I wasn't. There was too much on my mind to think about food.

Like my plan to leave and go save my pack.

After what felt like forever, the door opened, and light spilled into the room before darkness encompassed me again. I'd already retrieved my car keys from his jacket, and now all I had to do was wait for him to fall asleep.

My body stiffened as I heard the sounds of him getting ready for bed. The bathroom door shut, and light came from under the door. It sounded like he was brushing his teeth. Was he really going to sleep in the same bed as me?

The light turned off, and I shut my eyes and deepened my breathing. He stopped at the end of the bed, and then the mattress dipped as he lowered himself on the other side. His scent washed over me, pine with a hint of mint thanks to his toothpaste.

"Goodnight, bunny." He rolled over, and I resisted the urge to turn and look at him.

He wasn't that close to me, which was both a relief and a bit of a letdown. I suppressed my sigh.

He fell asleep quickly. As soon as a soft snore came from him, I slid out of bed and grabbed my shoes. If he woke up in the middle of my escape, he was going to lose his shit.

I waited until I was outside the door to put on my shoes. No one was in the main room and the lights were dimmed. I tip-toed down the stairs, flinching at the sound and wishing I wouldn't have put on my shoes yet.

I focused on the front door, my goal clear. I rushed to it, unlocked it, and nearly cried in frustration as it made a horrible squeaking sound. If they caught me, they'd never let me out of their sights again.

So far, I was undetected, and I just hoped I could make it into my car before they caught me. My plan was to park just outside pack territory and shift, if my body would let me. My wolf senses were better suited for being stealthy.

What the hell was I thinking? I wasn't suited for any of this. I'd just discovered I was a wolf, and now I was going to go on a rescue mission like I was some badass alpha boss bitch.

Climbing in my car, I wondered what Carly had meant about me being an alpha. There was only supposed to be one alpha in a pack, and now two wolves from completely different packs had said it.

My car started with a soft purr, and I quickly turned on the defroster and my windshield wipers. The snow was falling at a slant, but the visibility was still decent enough to drive. If I'd waited another half hour, the visibility would have been zero.

I was doing this, whether it was a good idea or not. My gut told me I needed to save my mates before it was too late.

CHAPTER FIVE

Eli

I'd fucked up. Without thinking out a better plan, I'd written the note and hidden the key at the bottom of the food. Dante and his minions—all who I once considered family—watched me closely, but not close enough.

Dante's plan to take over the pack was well thought out. He had enough wolves with weapons on his side that he could keep away those of us that would fight back. He'd also had enough forethought to buy dog food.

I couldn't stop the groan that escaped as I regained consciousness after Joseph had tied me up to a chair and knocked me out. It was the middle of the day and light streamed through the living room window; the trees teasing me with their gentle movement in the breeze.

The house was quiet besides the faint sounds of birds chirping outside. I considered shifting, but the ropes were tied tightly in several places that would leave my wolf bound to the chair as well. Plus, I had one last key hidden and shifting would ruin that.

"Look who's awake." Joseph's taunting voice drew closer, but I didn't dare turn my head. The smell of ham, swiss, and mustard on sourdough hit my nose, and I stifled a moan.

I was starving.

"No response? That's a shame. I was going to share my sandwich with you, but since you're ignoring me, I'll eat the whole thing myself." He set his plate down on the coffee table and then my chair was turned around so I was facing the couch instead of the window. "That's too nice of a view for a treasonous omega."

He picked up the plate and pinched a piece of crust off, holding it to my lips. Just as I was opening my mouth, he dropped the small morsel and laughed.

"I need food." My stomach panged in hunger. It must have been twenty-four hours since I last ate anything.

"You don't need anything, pretty boy." He sat down on the couch and took a big bite of the sandwich, shutting his eyes and moaning as he chewed.

As soon as I was free, I was going to kill him.

"Question." He set the sandwich down, and I couldn't help it, I was obsessed with the way the ham was piled and how his bite made the perfect indentation in the bread. "Did you really think Cole and the stray were going to escape?"

My eyes burned with tears and I swallowed down the lump that had formed. "I don't know what you're talking about."

"I think you do." Dante came from down the hall. I hadn't even heard a door open; I was so focused on not losing my shit. And the sandwich. I was focused on the sandwich. "Joseph, what are you doing? I told you to bring me his sister."

Joseph took another bite. "She's gone. Her and Manny have no tracking on them." Dante snatched the sandwich and plate from him and dropped them on the table.

I could have kissed Manny for making sure my sister got away safely. Dante had always had it out for her, even in human form. Omegas were supposed to be cherished, not treated like dog shit on the bottom of his boot.

"Where's Ivy?" They hadn't said a word about her, and I wondered where they had taken her. My worst fear was that she was dead or badly injured somewhere, scared and alone.

Dante turned his attention back to me and came close, pinching my chin roughly and moving my head from side to side to look at what I assumed were head wounds or bruising. I was so numb I didn't even feel them.

"Ivy's dead."

My wolf pushed forward, and my fangs descended. I whimpered and Dante squeezed my jaw harder.

"She has a set of lungs on her, let me tell you. Kept fighting until the very end."

I pushed back my wolf, unwilling to let him see how much turmoil brewed inside me. All the years of being the omega and stopping my wolf from putting my sister in her rightful place was paying off.

"What's wrong, omega? Did you think that was going to last? She was a parasite that was going to ruin this pack. It's bad enough Cole let the pack lose sight of itself."

"And you're not?" I spit on him, my saliva landing on his cheek. "You've forsaken the pack and all wolves."

He let go of me and wiped his face with the back of his forearm. He grinned and the blow he sent to the side of my head was so hard the chair fell sideways, slamming me into the floor.

~

Gasping for air, I woke as my body hit the hard floor. The cell door slammed shut, and the lock clicked into place. It had been a while since I'd been locked up, and I already wanted to claw my skin off.

"It's a real shame we couldn't get along, Elias." Dante wiped his hands on his jeans as I tried to sit up. "Now I have even more motivation to find that sister of yours."

My entire body ached, but that didn't stop me from pushing to my feet and trying to get to him, except there were bars in the way. "Why are you doing this?"

He lunged forward, grabbing me by the throat with both hands and dragging me close enough he could bite off my nose. "It's time for wolves to take their rightful place in this world."

He shoved me back, and I landed hard on my ass. "You won't get away with this."

Without another word, he and Joseph went up the stairs and slammed the door shut behind them. I sagged in relief that I was locked up instead of subjected to their abusive whims upstairs.

A whimper came from behind me, and I turned toward one of the other cages. Xander was in his wolf form again, his glossy eyes staring back at me.

"You're lucky they didn't kill you." Cole was slumped against the bars, his wound bleeding through the bandages.

He needed to have it cleaned and bandaged with medicine. All the moving around and lack of a comfortable resting place wasn't helping it either.

"He said he killed Ivy." Something about that thought felt wrong. I don't know how, but I still felt like she was alive.

"You really believe that?" Cole put his hand on Xander's head and rubbed it absently. Xander's eyes closed halfway, and I narrowed my eyes at Cole. "What's that look for?"

"Nothing." I used the bars to help me to my feet. I should have been the one comforting Xander, not him. What the hell was I even thinking? Xander wasn't mine, and I wasn't his. "We need to get out of here."

"We tried. They caught us." Cole's shoulders

slumped. "Xander shifted when he woke up and I can't convince him to shift back."

"Can you blame him?" I pulled down my pants. "Shut your eyes. Both of you."

"I've seen your dick plenty of times." Cole laughed and then groaned in pain. "Fuck, it hurts to laugh."

Xander let out a small growl and cocked his head to the side, watching me intently.

"Fine." I pulled myself out of my boxers and flipped my dick up to reveal a key taped underneath.

Cole hissed in a breath. "Stop. Laughing hurts." He put his hand over his stomach. "Smart, but how did you pull that off?"

"Their first mistake was locking me in my room after they took my computer." I peeled the tape, wincing as it pulled at the sensitive flesh. "They were smart enough to put someone outside the window."

"How many are there?"

"It's hard to say. At least ten, but they also are heavily armed. I overheard them talking about wanting to hold a pack meeting tonight, but with the storm rolling in, they can't." I held up the key in triumph and pulled my pants back up. "I couldn't quite figure out why he would keep us alive."

Xander shifted and sat up. "To make an example of us. If he just got rid of us right away, it would look more suspicious. Tonight is the perfect time to escape."

"Cole's too injured. We should wait." I took off my shirt and threw it across to them. "For you to sit on."

"I'll be fine. I'm better than I was earlier. I think Xander is right. If they are not calling a meeting, the storm is going to be bad." Cole winced as he lifted his body for Xander to slide the shirt underneath him. "We need to get out of here and find Ivy."

"What if she's-"

"She's not dead." Xander stopped me from even saying it.

"You can see the monitors better from that cage. We should wait until it's night and the snow is coming down hard," Cole suggested, ignoring the fact that we had no clue where Ivy was or what had happened to her. "Then we get the hell out of here."

It sounded like a horrible idea, but what choice did we have?

∽

NIGHT CAME, and it had grown eerily silent in the basement. The monitors had darkened as the sun had set, and the snow was falling hard enough that it was hard to make out anything.

"Are we really going to do this?" I stood and stretched. I was exhausted, but hopefully we'd soon be somewhere safe. I had no clue where we'd go, but there had to be members of the pack that weren't buying Dante's lies and deceit.

"Yes. I've been thinking. We'll get some tranquilizers from the med cabinet, grab a few instruments we can use as weapons, then go out through the house." Cole grunted as he stood. "If there's a lot of men, I'll distract them and you two run."

"We're not leaving you behind." I shook my head at

the idea. "We either all escape together or we all stay here."

"Cole's right. They will want to keep him the most. If none of us get away, we're screwed. One of us needs to make it to get help." Xander came to the bars, wrapping his hands around them.

"My sister has probably gotten help if she got away."

"But with the storm, who knows when they'll arrive. This is our opportunity, Eli." Xander stared at me intently, and I nodded. He was right. They were both right.

"If we get separated, we can meet at the treehouse and go from there. No one knows about it except us. And even if they did, they wouldn't guess that's where we were." Cole stood and picked up the shirt from the floor. "Let's do this."

I unlocked my cell as quietly as possible and stopped to listen for any sounds. When I heard none, I unlocked the other cell without a word before heading to the medical room. There were plenty of tranquilizers left, and I took two for each of us. Next, I cut off Cole's bandage and assessed his wound. It was healing, but slower than usual thanks to the poison and the situation we were in. "Why didn't you shift to your wolf to let it heal?" I put medicine over the angry flesh that I was sure would leave a scar and wrapped his wound.

"My wolf is barely holding it together. Can't let him be in control." Cole put his hand on my shoulder. "Promise me you'll run with Xander if things don't go well."

I shut my eyes, not wanting to think about what would happen if there was an army of our own waiting to take us down. "I promise."

"Let's do this." Cole pushed past me, taking two tranquilizers, and went back into the holding room and then up the stairs.

Xander was right behind him, and I brought up the rear. My body trembled with both fear and adrenaline. There was no way no one was in the house.

Cole tried the door, but it was locked. "Xander."

Xander moved in front of Cole, and with one swift kick, the door was open, and we rushed into the hall.

Joseph had been sleeping in a chair in the hall and jumped to his feet, but Xander hit him with a tranquilizer before he could fully react.

Cole and I followed him into the living room where two men who we thought were trustworthy pack mates jumped over the back of the couch. Xander dodged one who then set his sights on me.

For being injured, Cole advanced on them with a swiftness that was what made him the alpha. He dropped low, sweeping his leg out to knock down one of the men before hitting him with a tranquilizer right in the chest.

I swung at the man coming at me, taking a hit in the side, the pain reverberating through my body. I connected with his jaw, but that only pissed him off and he swung again. His fist was caught mid swing by Xander, who twisted his arm until it snapped.

Nausea rolled in my stomach at the sound of the

bone breaking, and the man cried out in pain before Xander knocked him out.

"Let's move. That probably woke up anyone sleeping in the rooms." Cole was already moving toward the back door, taking a detour around the island to grab a knife from the butcher's block.

Xander did the same, and I wrenched open the door. The snow was already a foot high.

We'd made it halfway across the yard when the sound of the roll up door on the den and shouts could be heard. I looked over my shoulder as three wolves came after us. We needed to shift.

"Split up! Xander, go with Eli." Before I could protest, Cole shifted and turned to the west.

"Damn it!" I slowed for a second, unsure what to do, and Xander took my hand. "We can't just let him sacrifice himself! They'll kill him!"

Xander was stronger than he looked and yanked me along as we got to the trees. "Where's this treehouse? We're of no use to them. I might be a beta myself, but I am in no condition to fight and neither are you."

"And he is?" My voice shook from fear and the cold.

"We'll be faster with our wolves." He let my hand go and shifted, proving me right by surging ahead.

The wolves chasing us veered after Cole, and I cursed. If we just followed behind them, we could take them unexpectedly.

But were there just the three or were there more lurking?

I shifted and caught up to Xander. Unable to

communicate with him, I nudged him in the neck with my nose and then ran for the treehouse.

No one else knew where it was as far as we knew. That was wishful thinking, but no one would think we would hide right in the middle of the territory if we were trying to escape.

When we reached the tree, I shifted and grabbed the rope pull, pulling the ladder down. Xander climbed up ahead of me, and as soon as we were inside, I raised the ladder again.

"Fuck. We're sitting ducks up here." Xander was already at one of the windows and opened it to look out. Cold air and snow flew in, and he slammed the wooden hatch shut. "This was a stupid idea."

"It'll be fine." I wasn't so sure of that and closed the wooden hatch on the floor. "We have a few blankets."

I frowned at the pile still on the floor from the other day and bent to pick them up. Cole hadn't come to get them, at least. The scents from our activities wafted from them, and I was struck with an overwhelming sense of loss.

"Hey." Xander put a hand on my shoulder. "It's going to be fine."

He took a blanket from me, and his eyes widened. He brought it to his nose and inhaled, his eyes darkening.

"We may have had some play time up here." I chuckled and wrapped the other blanket around myself. "Fuck, it's cold. Maybe we should shift."

He paced the length of the treehouse. "How's this going to work... the three of us with one woman?"

Teeth chattering, I watched as it took him four strides to walk from one side to the other. "That's a conversation we need to have with Cole."

"But you two already had a conversation, did you not?"

"That was when there were just two of us. We're best friends." I sat down on the floor and brought my knees to my chest, trying to create warmth. Wolf genetics only took you so far when you had bare skin exposed to the elements.

"I guess we need to get out of this situation first before we start fighting over her." He sat down next to me, shoulder to shoulder, and mimicked my pose.

"I don't think she'll let us fight over her. She has a best friend that has three boyfriends, so she's pretty unfazed by it all." My body was extremely aware of the length of his arm touching mine and I frowned. "I hope she doesn't want to choose, because she'll choose Cole, I just know it."

I didn't think it was possible for him to get closer, but he wrapped his arm around my shoulder, covering part of me with his blanket.

"There are a lot of things you offer that Cole doesn't." He chuckled. "Like a longer dick."

My face heated, and I ducked my head, covering myself under the blanket. Jesus Christ, why did he have to admit to thinking about the size of my dick, and why did it make me blush?

"I was kidding." He pulled the blanket back and smirked at me. "Well, kidding about Ivy selecting a mate based on dick size. Not about... you know what? Never mind."

We sat huddled together for I don't know how long. I was starting to really worry about Cole. He should have been here by now if he got away.

"Have you been with him?" Xander asked, searching my face.

"What?" I furrowed my brows.

"With Cole? Have you been with him?"

I nearly choked on my saliva. "What? No."

"Have you ever wanted to?" What the heck was going on?

A whole-body tremor shook me, and I wished we were as hot-blooded as the movies always made us seem. Our wolves could handle the cold, but we could still freeze our nuts off in our human forms.

Xander laid down and opened his blanket. "Come here."

I looked at him wide-eyed. "What?"

"Is that your favorite word? Come here. We can make a burrito to stay warm." He didn't even seem to be that cold.

"I don't know." Another tremor shook my body, and I laid down in front of him. I needed the warmth, and he was offering.

He wrapped his arm around my waist and pulled me closer, pulling the edge of his blanket around me.

"Don't be so tense." He breathed against my ear, and I shivered, but not from the cold. "I don't bite."

But maybe a small part of me wanted him to.

CHAPTER SIX

Cole

My entire body ached as I ran through the foot-deep snow, leading my former pack mates, and now enemies, away from Eli and Xander. I knew what was going to happen the second we broke through the basement door. Dante wouldn't leave either escape route uncovered.

If sacrificing myself to save Eli was the last thing I did in my life, then the pain was worth it. *But what about Ivy?*

I had to believe she was okay and had gotten away. She had nearly escaped from me, so getting free of Dante's clutches would be a walk in the park. Unfortunately, he not only had guns, but tranquilizer guns. It was hard to outrun a speeding bullet.

She couldn't be dead. I could still sense she was alive in my soul.

I passed a tree that I was sure I had passed before and turned, knowing they were gaining on me. The visibility was dropping by the minute, and I could barely see. It was going to save me or lead to my untimely death.

Something hit my flank, sending me flying off course and right into a tree. I scrambled to get up, but my legs gave out, my sensitive belly hitting the cold snow with a flash of pain. Darkness flooded my vision, and I felt like I was being pulled down into the ground.

My father circled me, baring his teeth as I pulled myself to my feet, considering my next move. I was just shy of my eighteenth birthday and he wanted to ensure that when I took my place as his lead beta, that I could hold my own. Not only that, but that when I eventually took his place, that I could maintain it.

"Don't hesitate. That gives them time to think." He lunged for me and I was unprepared, taking a nip to my back leg as I tried to get out of the way.

Doing as he instructed, I didn't think about the sting of the cut. Instead, I spun around and jumped on his back.

"That's it!" He threw me off. "But not good enough."

"Can we take a break? We've been doing this for an hour." I needed water and maybe a rabbit.

"Those that wish to take your position in the pack won't care that you're tired and hungry." He circled me again. "They will come at you when you're at your weakest. You can't ever stop pushing back."

"No one in the pack even comes close to the strength we

have." It was true, too. Even my father's current head beta and his son were nothing compared to us.

"Sometimes the weakest believe themselves to be strong and will stop at nothing to get what they want. If the weakest challenges you, do not hesitate to kill them."

I chuffed. "It will be a cold day in hell if someone challenges one of us."

"Cole?" Ivy's voice was in my head and I jerked awake.

"Ivy?" I was met with silence.

Clawing at the snow, I tried to stand. The faint sound of footsteps drew my attention to the three wolves approaching. I didn't think I'd been passed out that long if they were just now approaching me.

Fuck. Do it for Ivy. Get up and fight for her.

I got to my feet, but felt like I might collapse again at any moment. I hadn't given the wound proper time to heal, and whatever poison Dante had used was still in my system. My body didn't even feel like my own.

With the small bit of strength I had left, I surged forward, Dante doing the same. He had the upper hand, with two wolves at his side, but I would die fighting. It was all I could do now that they had me cornered.

Before we collided, Dante was suddenly gone. A yelp came from somewhere nearby, and then the sounds of two fighting wolves filled the silence. Had Xander and Eli not listened to me?

There was no way either of them could take Dante on their own, but maybe together they could put him down or hurt him enough for him to flee. But then there were two other wolves to contend with.

I skidded to a halt, my legs feeling like they were going in ten different directions, and the two other wolves circled me. From the look in their eyes, they were unsure of what they should do. I couldn't talk to them—which meant Dante had enough wolves from the pack following him that my alpha status was no more—but I pleaded with my eyes. Did they even know what Dante had done to me?

"Run." Ivy? She was nearby and alive. Relief flooded me and my eyes stung with tears. I was so fucking glad she was okay.

Growling, I lunged for one of the wolves, our bodies colliding and teeth biting at each other. He fought with uncertainty, and I put him on his back in no time, despite being at my weakest. But then again, he wasn't trying to dominate me.

There was hope yet for me getting my pack back.

Each inhale of air burned as I backed off him after he submitted. I looked at the other wolf and now there were two... no, four of him. Stumbling to the side, I barely stayed on my feet as several Dantes appeared next to them.

I blinked hard, trying to clear my vision. Where did the other wolf go that attacked him?

A vicious warning came from beside me, sending a chill down my spine. Everything was happening in slow motion, and I couldn't make sense of it. When had Ivy gotten here?

She crept forward, her teeth bared. Dante stood his

ground, but the other two wolves backed up, tucking their tails. She snarled louder, and Dante snarled back, but without as much gusto as he usually had.

He was bleeding from his neck and had a cut on his nose, the blood dripping like a slow leak onto the snow. Dizziness washed over me, and I felt myself falling right as Ivy lunged forward. Dante turned and ran, Ivy hot on his heels.

I fell into the cold, white oblivion. Finally, I could rest.

CHAPTER SEVEN

Ivy

The taste of Dante's blood was still in my mouth as he ran away with the two other wolves flanking him. I had jumped on his back and bit into his neck again. My aim was to kill him, but he was larger than me and I still didn't know what the hell I was doing.

I bit into some snow and spit it out again, trying to get the taste of him out of my mouth. I needed to get back to Cole. I had a feeling Dante wouldn't be back anytime soon, but the quicker we could get away, the better.

How was I going to get back to my car? It had to be two miles away, if not more. I wasn't exactly the best at directions, so it was an estimate. I'd barely found my way to the house and then picked up the scent of my mates. I didn't even really know how to communicate with them. I just pushed what I wanted to say toward them and hoped for the best.

When I couldn't taste blood anymore, I ran back in the direction I came, sniffing the air for any scent that would lead me back to Cole. All I smelled was snow.

The snow was still falling hard, but the wind had let up, giving me more visibility. Plus, my wolf was better at seeing than I was in human form.

I felt like I was walking in circles. All the trees looked the same to me.

Spotting Cole, I rushed to him. He looked like he was dead, and my heart skipped a beat. I licked at his snout, making small whimpering noises to try to wake him up. I put my head on his chest and even though it rose slightly, his breaths were shallow.

Don't die, please.

I laid down next to him, putting my snout over his. How was I going to get him to safety? Where were Xander and Eli? I had smelled them when I got to the house and figured out which direction they'd gone in, but now the only thing I could smell was Cole.

"Can you hear me?" I hit what felt like a brick wall trying to communicate with Cole. It wasn't something I'd experienced before when talking that way.

I thought of Eli, thinking of his dark brown hair neatly slicked back, his dark eyes burning into my soul. *"Eli, can you hear me?"*

"Ivy? Where are you?" Excitement filled me that it worked, even though I could barely hear him. Was there a volume button for wolf thoughts?

"I'm with Cole. He's hurt bad." I nuzzled his neck, inhaling the scent I hadn't realized I'd grown to love. *"Dante's gone for now. I injured him."*

"We're in the treehouse. Cole was supposed to meet us here. We'll come find you."

"No. I'll come to you. I'm not sure I know what direction you're in though." Getting to my feet, I looked around at the trees obscured by snow and the darkness of night. My night vision was excellent, but it wasn't like I could see through fast falling snow.

"You shouldn't be that far away. Focus on my voice and it'll lead you in the right direction."

"I'll try. Tell me a story so I can figure out how to."

"Once upon a time..." I snorted and concentrated on his voice.

I could feel which direction his voice was coming from, relief washing over me. It wasn't the time to think about how cool it was to be pulled in a direction just from someone's voice. I needed to get Cole somewhere safe.

The cold hit my body like I was submerged in an ice bath as I shifted. I scooped up Cole as carefully as possible and began trudging through the snow, my feet not as cold as I thought they would be.

Cole wasn't as heavy as I expected, but then again, I was stronger than I had been before. I continued walking for what felt like forever, listening to Eli retell *Little Red Riding Hood*. I didn't like the story now that I was a wolf myself.

His voice was getting stronger and stronger in my mind the longer I walked. *"I'm close, I think."*

"We opened the hatch and put down the ladder. I can't smell you though. The snow covers scents pretty well."

"I smelled what direction you'd run in when I got to the house."

"Our scent is strong there. You probably just picked it up going into the woods. We took the same path we normally do. Or you just have super wolf scenting abilities."

"Is that a thing?" I laughed out loud, the sound deafening in the silent forest.

"I have no clue, but I think anything is possible with you."

I adjusted my hold on Cole and looked up at the trees, spotting the treehouse not far away. I practically ran to the base of the tree where the ladder was waiting for me. Eli's head popped over the side of the opening. It was still dark and snowing at a slant, but I could make out his worried expression.

"I'll come down there and carry him."

Before Eli could climb down, I heaved Cole onto my shoulders, wrapping my arm around him. Hopefully, I wouldn't drop him, but if I did, there was snow on the ground to cushion the fall.

I started climbing, panting with the exertion of carrying nearly two hundred pounds of wolf up the ladder. Not too long ago, I'd squatted just shy of that, and this was kind of the same, wasn't it?

Or maybe it was just my new wolf abilities and my adrenaline carrying me up the ladder.

I got near the top, where Eli and Xander reached out and grabbed onto Cole, pulling him to safety. I climbed into the treehouse right behind them, and Eli secured the ladder where it couldn't be seen and shut the hatch.

I collapsed onto my back with a groan. My entire body felt frozen, but I'd made it. I waved Eli and Xander off as they made a move for me. "Take care of him first. I'm fine."

"Where have you been?" Eli wrapped a blanket around Cole, and Xander sat near my feet and rubbed them. They prickled as sensation returned to them.

"Dante threw me in the river." I blew on my hands, trying to warm them up. "And then the West Arbor Pack found me."

"Did they hurt you?" Eli sounded angry, which was an odd emotion coming from him. I'd only known him for about a week, but he didn't seem like he angered easily.

I propped myself up on my forearms. "They didn't hurt me. I guess you could say they helped me. But I ran over Silas's motorcycle if that makes you feel better." Sitting up, I took the blanket that Xander was holding out to me, wrapping it around myself. "Are you two okay?"

Xander shrugged. "Cole took the brunt of their anger. Eli got a little roughed up, but he's healed." Xander took my feet again and began massaging the arch. I nearly rolled my eyes into the back of my head; it felt so good. "We shouldn't have left Cole alone, but he separated from us before we could stop him. Even injured he's fast."

"He wouldn't have had it any other way. He's stubborn." Eli sat next to me and wrapped his arms around me, rubbing my back and my arms. "You said you hurt Dante?"

"He and two other wolves were about to attack Cole, so I went for his throat. I got a few good bites in, enough to make him run with his tail between his legs. The other two didn't seem like they really wanted to fight us." I put my head on his shoulder, his soothing voice making me sleepy. "We need to get out of here sooner rather than later. I parked my car off the highway, just to the side of the main road."

"That's about three miles away. In this weather we might not to make it there without being detected or freezing to death in our human forms. I guess we could take turns carrying Cole while the other two are wolves."

Xander let go of my feet and crawled to the other side of me, wrapping his arms around me too. I was in a wolf sandwich, and I wasn't complaining any. "What can we do then?"

"About three-quarters of a mile away is our fire station of sorts. We have some all-terrain vehicles, large trucks, and a helicopter." Eli chuckled. "We could fly out of here."

"No way. I'm not going in a helicopter." Xander's arm was around my waist, and he squeezed. "Who would fly it?"

"Well, Cole isn't going to." I looked at him lying at my feet. His breaths seemed to have normalized, and he was snoring lightly. "He was pretty out of it when I found him. He was stumbling around like he was drunk."

"We need to let him rest. He's gone too long without healing completely and keeps reinjuring himself. He didn't want to rest; I think because he was worried Dante had…"

It got quiet as I let them snuggle against me and warm me up. I was at a loss for words. They probably thought I was dead. Hell, I thought I had died at one point.

"I'm here now, though. We're all together again." I bit my lip. "I need to tell you that Silas is my mate too."

"Who's this Silas guy you keep talking about?" Xander had slid the blanket off one of my shoulders and was rubbing his stubbled cheek against my bare arm.

"Silas is the alpha of the other pack. He and Cole used to be best friends until the alpha was killed and their fathers split into two packs. I don't know him that well." Eli pulled back and looked at my face. "How do you feel about him being a mate?"

"Honestly, I haven't given it much thought." There were too many other things to worry about, like Dante trying to stage a coup and how I was going to save my men. "I haven't really thought about it."

"We should get some rest, so when the storm lets up a bit more we can make a move." Eli laid down next to Cole, throwing an arm over him. "Get close to him. The body heat will help him heal."

So that was what we did. Three naked humans cuddled up to a wolf that was growling in his sleep.

I SLEPT hard as warmth engulfed me from all sides. Xander was wrapped around my back, and Cole was in front of me. My hands were buried in the fur around his neck, with my head resting on my arm. I never knew the rough wood floor of a treehouse could be so comfortable. But what made it comfortable was them.

Something wet slid across my cheek, and I stirred, trying to decide if it was worth it to wake up completely to figure out what it was. It happened again, and I cracked my eyes open, finding Cole wide awake and licking my face.

Moving my hands to my face, I blocked him from assaulting me with his tongue again. It didn't gross me out, but it was kind of weird.

"Stop it, you mangy mutt," I whispered, trying to keep from waking Eli and Xander. "You should be sleeping still. You need to heal."

He shifted back to his human form, blinking back at me and bringing a hand to my cheek. "You healed me."

My eyes widened, and I looked down at his torso where an angry scar marred his once smooth abdomen. I slid my fingers over the translucent skin, and he broke out in goosebumps.

"What do you mean I healed you?" I frowned, my mind already whirring with the implications. Wolf shifters didn't heal others as far as I knew. So, what the fuck was I?

His hand trailed down my arm to entwine our fingers, and he brought them to his lips, placing a gentle kiss on them. "All I felt was this intense warmth spreading through my body and pooling in my gut where the wound was. When I opened my eyes, your hands were glowing faintly." He pulled our hands away from his mouth and examined the palm. "I don't know how it's possible, but it happened."

"Maybe it was just your fast healing, and you were dreaming. Eli said that cuddling up next to you would help you heal." I examined my hand, wondering if it could be true.

"No, I'm pretty sure it was you. It should've taken me a lot longer given the state I was in. I was on the brink of death and you brought me back." He leaned in and pressed his lips to mine. "Thank you."

Heat rose to my cheeks. "What does it mean?"

My entire existence was a big fat question mark. I just wanted answers, but the questions kept on mounting. It was suffocating. As soon as I saw Silas again, I was going to ask him more about his father and why he would pay my social worker a large sum of money. I would have asked Cole, but he had almost died, and I didn't want to overwhelm him.

Then there was the photo.

"Right now, it doesn't matter. What matters is that we get away from here and come up with a plan to get the pack back." Cole started to sit up, and I pushed him down with my hand.

"Let's rest a little longer." I was so comfortable surrounded by the three of them that I didn't want to move.

Eli had moved to the other side of Xander at some point. There was something going on there, and I should have been jealous, but I wasn't. If I was going to be with three, possibly four men, I wasn't about to say the swords couldn't cross. I *wanted* them to.

His skin still had goosebumps as I rubbed his arm. "Are you cold?"

"No. I'm actually a little hot." Cole's eyes trailed down my body and then met my eyes again.

He looked past me at Xander pressed up against my back, his head buried in my hair. "You really want this? The three of us?" Cole's brows furrowed as he studied my face.

I trailed a finger over the tattoo on Cole's pec. He shut his eyes and then hummed low in his throat.

"I want to see where it goes. My best friend makes it work with three guys and has for seven years. I don't see why I can't make it work with four." I grimaced as his eyes opened and widened. "Who knows, there might even be more."

"What do you mean by four?" He put his hand over mine to stop me from tracing around his nipple, which was a solid pebble.

"Turns out that Silas is also my mate." A low growl came from his throat, and I put a finger over his lips. "I didn't do anything with him. He saved me from the river, I escaped, I ran over his motorcycle, and that was it."

Cole studied my face for a moment. His tongue came out of his mouth and licked my finger before he sucked it into his mouth. I drew in a sharp breath as he swirled his tongue around it and then released it.

"I don't think now is really the best time to get freaky." I wasn't just saying that because all three of them were with me. We were stuck in a treehouse during a snowstorm, hiding from a psychopath beta wolf who thought he could take over the pack.

But that didn't stop my body from coming alive and need to swirl in my stomach, moving south to settle between my legs. I felt like I was always horny now, and it didn't matter if I was in a life-or-death situation.

Just as I was about to get up and stop what was happening to my body, Xander's hand clamped down on my hip as if he sensed it. He hadn't even lifted his face from my hair, but I could feel his breath against the back of my neck.

Cole's eyes traveled down my body again and he grinned. "Seems like the perfect time to get reacquainted with each other's bodies. It'll give us a little endorphin and serotonin boost too. We need it after everything. We thought we'd lost you." He cupped my cheek again and leaned in, our lips connecting and my body detonating with need.

Xander's hand lightly trailed up and down my side, sending shivers down my spine. I felt him hardening against the small of my back and my pulse skyrocketed. We barely knew each other, but that didn't matter.

Hell, I barely knew Cole and Eli, but deep inside, I knew them better than anyone else. They were a part of me, and my body craved all three of them.

Cole kissed along my jaw to my neck where he sucked the skin lightly. I shuddered and shut my eyes, giving myself over to the sensations of their touches.

Xander's hand trailed from my hip to my pelvic bone, where he traced a circle with his finger. If his aim was to drive me crazy, it was working. He pushed my hair out of the way, and his lips glided across my shoulders.

"Please, no teasing." I wrapped my fingers around Cole's erection and began pumping my hand, drawing a groan that was loud enough to wake the dead.

Xander's lips brushed my ear and his hand inched down between my legs, cupping me in a possessive way that nearly made me orgasm on the spot. "But teasing is my favorite thing."

His finger moved down my slit and rubbed across my entrance. Every nerve ending was firing in my body, the pressure mounting in my core.

I'd wondered if Cole was going to accept another guy being in the mix, but he clearly didn't mind because his mouth closed around my nipple. My grip on him tightened as Xander finally slid a finger in my pussy and then quickly added a second.

"Need your dick," I rasped, grabbing Cole's hair with my other hand.

Xander's hand stilled, and I felt him smile against my neck. "What's the magic word?"

"Fuck." I bucked my hips, trying to seek relief. "Please."

Cole began kissing his way down my body, my hand slipping from his cock as Xander's chest rumbled behind me in a laugh. He removed his fingers and the tip of his dick pressed against my entrance. As much as it made me burn up inside, the teasing only made me wetter.

He pushed into me suddenly, filling me with a

thrust that caused me to gasp. Or maybe that was from Cole moving my leg to open me up and watching as Xander's cock slid in and out of my tight channel.

A groan came from behind Xander, and Eli mumbled something unintelligible. I wanted to see him, but I was not in a good position to unless I had suddenly developed a neck like an owl's.

"Eli?" He grunted in response. "Come over here so I can see you."

Cole's tongue flicked my clit, and I gasped. Hands down, the treehouse was my new favorite place.

Eli stood and then lowered to his knees in front of me, his fist wrapping around his cock. He rubbed his thumb over the head before he began fucking his hand.

Xander's thrusts quickened and his hand tightened on my hip. I cried out as my orgasm rolled through me like a freight train, my legs trembling and my ears ringing as Xander came, his groans of pleasure muffled against my back.

I reached up to take over for Eli, but Xander's hand had already found its way to cover his. Eli was still, his breath catching and thighs trembling in front of me.

Cole kissed my inner thigh and sat up on his knees, moving forward and placing my hand on him again. He thrust his hips, his eyes on the scene playing out before us.

The moment Eli let go of his cock, giving Xander full access to it, Xander scraped his teeth against my shoulder. "Take him in your mouth, Ivy."

I propped myself up on my forearm and let Xander guide Eli to my mouth, taking him until my lips touched his hand wrapped around the base of Eli's dick. He was harder than I'd ever felt a man be.

"So fucking hot." Cole's hot cum spilled onto my hand as he came.

Eli thrust into my mouth, his velvety skin hot against my lips. He gasped and then exploded, his salty cum sliding down my throat. I sucked him until he pulled away, collapsing back on his ass.

"I hope I didn't push him too far," Xander mumbled against my shoulder, wrapping his arm around me.

I patted his hand. "I think he's blissed out right now." Eli covered his face with his hands as he laid down on his back, his chest heaving. "Just give him time to process."

Hell, I needed time to process. How was I ever going to have normal sex again?

CHAPTER EIGHT

Ivy

After cleaning up with the blankets, we climbed out of the treehouse. My legs were still shaking as we set off toward the fire station. The wind had died down significantly, but the snow was still lightly falling. Dante would probably try to find us soon, so we needed to be quick.

We shifted and followed Cole, who seemed to be perfectly healthy again. I didn't know what to think about him saying I had healed him. That wasn't something wolves normally did, at least from my understanding. Now wasn't the time to think about it, though.

It was hard to tell with the snow and the cover of the trees, but the sky was turning from black to a dark gray. I was still getting used to my wolf's vision, which was much wider than a human's, and the images were crisper. My brain was overloaded with the new perspective my body gave me.

My stomach protested as we ran, and my mind drifted to the thought of deer.

No.

Now was not the time to think about eating any more Bambis. I needed to eat though. *Maybe if we happen upon one, I can have a little nibble.*

"A nibble of what?" Cole asked. Had I transmitted my thought to him? I didn't mean to.

"Uh... a nibble of deer." I ran faster to catch up with him. *"I'm hungry, and I'm sure all of you are too."*

"Whoa. Why can I hear you?" Xander ran up behind me, leaving Eli slightly behind us. *"I can't hear Cole."*

"Apparently, I'm an alpha. We haven't had much time to explore why Cole and Eli can communicate with me. Maybe it's because I'm mates with you all." I would just add it to my list of giant life questions I needed an answer to.

"Does that mean I'm in your pack?"

"I don't know what the hell it means, honestly." And I didn't really care. All I wanted was to get somewhere safe and preferably with food. *"I haven't had time to check to see if it transfers to anybody else or to Silas."*

Maybe it was some kind of special mate connection activated by sex or a show of dominance. I hadn't put Xander on his back, but Xander also was the only one who didn't have a pack.

The building we were seeking came into view, and we slowed down to assess the situation. We needed to be careful in case Dante had men staked out. The East

Arbor Pack was large, and Dante's reach could only go so far in such a short period. Especially since he had to cancel his pack meeting because of the snowstorm.

We shifted as we got to the door, and it surprised me how easy and seamless it had become to go back and forth between my two physical states. My wolf and I felt like we were the same now.

As soon as we opened the door and stepped inside, heat washed over us. It felt so good to be in a room with central heat. While it had been warm under the blankets in the treehouse, this was a different type of warmth that permeated the body.

The inside of the building was dark besides a few dim lights evenly spaced along the brick walls. There were three giant trucks that were much larger than regular fire engines, a water tanker truck, a helicopter, and a trailer with all-terrain vehicles. It was impressive for belonging to a pack of wolves.

"Ryan is probably still sleeping. He's a heavy sleeper, but let's get out of here quickly." Cole pressed a button on the wall and the giant door slid open. He went to a set of hooks and grabbed a pair of keys.

"I really don't know about this whole flying thing." Xander took a pair of pants that Eli handed him and tugged them on. I wondered if someone's job was to check all their clothing caches and restock when they ran low. "The last time I was in a helicopter..."

He got a faraway look in his eye, and my heart clenched. I didn't know what had happened to him to bring him to us, but whatever it was had been traumatic.

"Cole is an excellent pilot. It's really the only way to get out of here quickly and without them following us." I took a pair of pants and a shirt from Eli and pulled them on. It seemed pointless to get dressed since it seemed all we did was shift and ruin our clothes. It was something we needed to work on. "I admit that at first, I thought he was full of shit about being able to fly a helicopter, but he's really quite good."

"So, you admit that I know what I'm doing." Cole smirked and opened the pilot's side door. He started to climb in, but a door opened, and a man with a long beard came out, rubbing his eyes.

"Cole?" The man stopped dead in his tracks and stared at Cole with wide eyes. "I thought they locked you up for killing... the woman." His eyes landed on me.

"Well, it turns out that I didn't kill *the woman* and Dante's a liar." Cole handed Eli the keys and stepped toward the man who I assumed was Ryan. "Is that what he told everybody?"

"He sent out a pack email last night telling us he was taking over as alpha because you'd murdered Ivy for challenging you." He looked me up and down. "What is this? Why are you taking the helicopter?"

Cole put his hand on the man's shoulder. "We're getting away from here for now. But I'll be back once we figure out what we're dealing with. Don't tell Dante that we were here, or that we took the helicopter."

"But…"

I stepped forward, already annoyed he had believed Dante. "When the storm clears and the sun shines again, whose side are you going to be on?" My hands formed fists against my sides, the anger I felt for Dante threatening to spill over onto this man. "Are you going to be on the rightful alpha's side or on a treasonous beta's side? A beta who shot and poisoned your alpha and tied a woman up and threw her in the river?"

The man's jaw ticked, and he looked at me seriously. "I'll kill him myself."

"Not yet. We don't know how many people are involved, and he's already caused enough deaths." I didn't know the three wolves he had killed already, but my heart ached for them and their families.

He nodded, and Cole cocked his head to the side, observing our interaction. I knew what was running through his head because it was running through mine too. The pack members were responding to me as if I was their leader.

Feeling the need to lighten the mood, I cleared my throat. "Do you have any food that we can take with us?"

Cole chuckled and put his arm around my waist. "Yeah, get the woman some food before she kills another deer."

He followed the man, which put me on edge, but he came back a few moments later, carrying a bag of beef jerky, a can of nuts, and a large bottle of water.

Eli started the helicopter and drove it out into the snow. I was suddenly hit with nerves. Not because we were flying, but because of where we had decided to fly to.

The West Arbor Pack was the closest, and with me acting as a neutral party, we could use their help to get our own pack back. They also had access to the server Eli needed to protect the pack's assets and to track down his sister. The nearest pack after them was too far away.

Xander stood off to the side, shaking his head as he watched the blades of the helicopter spin.

"Are you going to be okay?" I took his hand as we walked out to the helicopter, the snow instantly freezing my feet. "We can have a little snack in the back while we let Cole and Eli navigate. How does that sound?"

Xander had retreated into himself, and his gaze was glossy, staring straight ahead at nothing. He nodded briefly and allowed me to lead him to the back door of the helicopter. We strapped in and took the snacks from Cole.

We lifted off, Eli looking back at Xander's hand clutching mine for dear life across the space between our seats. He gave us a reassuring smile before turning forward again, the sky in front of us a mix of dark grays and whites.

After letting go of Xander's hand once we were moving toward our destination, I opened up the bag of beef jerky and offered him a piece. He stared at it as if he wasn't seeing it at all.

Since we didn't have headsets and yelling would be too distracting for Cole, who was navigating during a snowstorm, I focused on talking to Xander through my thoughts. *"It might help to busy yourself with something."* I took a bite of the dried meat and groaned. *"It's no deer, but it'll do."*

Xander looked over at me and blinked. *"You eat deer?"*

I shrugged. *"My wolf seems to like them a lot, even though I would rather not kill them. Cole makes some mean venison too."*

"Deer are sacred." He shook his head and stared past me out the window. *"Some packs don't believe they are, but mine did."*

"Then what should I eat?" I popped a few cashews in my mouth and shut my eyes. I really couldn't stop thinking about deer.

"Anything except deer." He reached over and took the can of nuts from me, appearing to have returned to normal, or as normal as he could be. *"My dad always told me that eating a deer was equivalent to flipping off the gods. It's what I grew up believing."*

"The gods?" I popped a brow. *"Like Poseidon and shit?"*

"We're about to land. Hold on, it's going to be a little rough." Cole interrupted our conversation, his voice loud over the sounds of the blades, and the helicopter shook like it was hitting turbulence.

I knew it was normal depending on the conditions, but Xander didn't and dropped the nuts, spilling them all over the floor. He gripped his seat and shut his eyes.

I unhooked my belt and sat on his lap, wrapping an arm around his neck so I wouldn't fall. *"Hey, you're okay. I'm right here."*

His eyes opened, and all I saw was the inner turmoil that was plaguing him. *"They took us in a helicopter."*

"We aren't them." I brushed my lips across his and he

relaxed a little, his arms coming around me instead of clutching the seat.

There were so many things I wanted to ask him, but landing in enemy territory wasn't the best time. I hoped with me as a buffer, Silas and Cole could put aside their differences until we took care of Dante.

We landed with a jolt, causing me to almost fly off Xander's lap. He tightened his arms around me and shut his eyes as the helicopter powered down.

"Sorry. It's harder to land in snow. I want you three to stay in here." Cole unhooked his belt, letting it fly into the seat with more force than necessary.

Looking out the front window, I saw what had gotten his panties in a knot. Standing right outside the door of the building was a shirtless Silas, with four others behind him.

I rolled my eyes and slid off Xander's lap as Cole jumped out of the helicopter and trudged to the front of it to engage in a macho stare off with Silas.

"What are you doing?" Eli unhooked his belt as I moved into the front seat and opened the pilot's door. "He said to stay here."

"All he's going to do is start a fight that is completely unnecessary." I slid out, flinching as my feet hit the snow. I needed a foot rub after all the snow walking without shoes I'd been doing.

As soon as I was outside the helicopter, I heard both men snarling at each other. I walked around to the front to stand next to Cole.

Silas narrowed his eyes at me. "Bunny, what the hell are you doing? I thought you were inside!" He crossed his arms over his naked chest and walked forward, drawing an even more feral sound from Cole.

"Stop calling me that." I was okay with nicknames, but bunnies were weak, and I was not.

"Cole doesn't have permission to be in my territory." Silas stopped four feet away and looked Cole up and down with disgust. "You've seen better days, my friend."

"I'm not your friend, and it's interesting you're commenting on my appearance when you look like you forgot what a shaver was." Cole gestured to his own face that was sporting stubble. "Nice place you have here. All the spots at the pound full?"

"Okay, guys. Let's stop being assholes to each other. Silas, we need a place to stay and help to get the pack back. If you don't want to help, fine. Let us borrow a vehicle and we'll go to my house. I have plenty of space for them."

"Them?" He looked at the helicopter as Xander and Eli climbed out. "What the hell were you thinking, leaving during a blizzard to go on a rescue mission? You could have been killed! That sad excuse for a beta already tried to kill you once."

"I wouldn't call the snowstorm a blizzard." I stepped forward and Cole reached out to take my arm, but I shook him off. I was close enough to Silas to see the amusement in his blue eyes at me brushing off Cole. "Are you going to help us or not?"

"What's in it for me?" His eyes danced with mischief, and a small smirk formed on his lips.

"The satisfaction of knowing you helped your

mate." I gave his cheek a pat and stepped back. "Plus, don't you want to help take down Dante?"

"You bet your ass I do." Silas's gaze went back to Cole. "This is my house. My rules. My men."

Cole stepped forward with another growl. I'd never heard so much growling in my life, but I guessed it was par for the course since we were wolves. "You forget which one of us outranks the other."

Silas threw his head back and laughed. "Says the alpha who let his mate get thrown into a river."

Whatever thread Cole was holding onto severed and he surged forward, shoving Silas's chest. They met head on, circling each other like... wolves.

"For Christ's sake." I bent down and scooped up some snow as the two of them began wrestling like teenage boys.

They weren't throwing punches yet, but they were trying to throw each other to the ground. I formed a snowball and threw it at Silas's head. His eyes snapped to me and he was mowed down to the ground by Cole.

"Maybe we should just leave them out here." Eli sounded like he was enjoying the show. "They can't hurt each other too much with their fists, and I'm getting cold."

Bone, Rover, and two other men I had been introduced to but forgot their names, were standing by the door looking bored and half asleep. It was probably around seven in the morning.

I scooped up more snow just as Silas rolled so Cole was under him. I took that as my opportunity to move in. Pulling Silas's sweatpants away from his ass, I dropped the handful of snow in.

He screeched and everyone, even Xander, laughed. He was off of Cole in less than a second, pawing at his ass. The snow was already wetting the back of his sweatpants.

"You'll pay for that." He charged at me, and I squealed, turning to run.

I didn't make it very far before I was tackled into the snow, the cold fluff hitting me from all sides and Silas's warm body pressing into mine. My laughter quickly faded as his hot breath fanned against my ear.

"I should spank your ass for that." It sounded like a promise, and I had the undeniable urge to squeeze my thighs together as my body became hyperaware that his dick was pressed against my ass. "Would you like that?"

His question ended on a high note as he was ripped off me.

"What the fuck is wrong with you?" Xander's voice boomed in the silence. "You could have hurt her!"

I sat up, wiping snow off my face. "I'm fine. He was just messing around."

Xander had Silas by the throat, and with inhuman strength, picked him up and slammed him into the front of the helicopter. Silas was trying to get free, but Xander was stronger than he looked.

"Xander, stop." Eli pulled at his arm, but Xander was focused on Silas.

The meanest growl I'd ever heard came from Xander, and then he threw Silas to the ground. Xander walked away from us, his back heaving. Eli followed but stayed a safe distance away.

"Always causing problems." Cole made a tsking sound and reached out to help me up. "Xander was a beta in his old pack, maybe he'd be an alpha here in your lame-"

"That's enough." An unfamiliar raspy voice came from the doorway of the building.

There was an old man standing there, his hair cut short and silver with age and a mean scowl on his face.

I brushed the snow from my clothes and watched him carefully as Silas's men parted for him to come out into the snow. His eyes were the same blue as Silas's. It couldn't be his father though; he was much older than the man in the picture had been.

"Pops, we were just having some fun." Silas stood up and shook off all the snow that was covering him before rubbing his throat.

"Boy, don't you lie to me. You've been picking fights since the day you were born." The man looked around at us. His eyes stopped on me and a flicker of something was gone before I could name it. "Stop acting like children and get your asses inside."

Silas let out a defeated breath of air and followed him in without a word.

I looked back at Eli and Xander, Eli motioning for us to leave them. Cole cleared his throat. "Let's go inside. Eli will take care of Xander."

"Maybe we should..." I wanted to take care of Xander.

"It's Eli's job to make sure the pack is mentally

healthy." He put his arm around my shoulder and started leading me inside.

"Who was that old man?" I whispered as we approached the door. "He was kind of scary."

"Silas's grandfather."

Maybe he'd have some answers to who my father was.

CHAPTER NINE

Xander

I had thought I was going to be okay until I stepped foot in the helicopter. The memories had flooded back like someone was shooting off an assault rifle, giving me no chance to escape. They'd taken everything from me, and they probably wouldn't hesitate to do it again.

If they ever found me... I wasn't sure I would survive another day of their torture.

Ivy had distracted me enough, but then the asshole who looked like he wanted to be on *Sons of Anarchy* tackled my girl, and I lost it.

I had to protect her, to prove to her that I could take care of her if they ever came.

The East Arbor Pack was bigger than my own, or

what used to be my own. I was certain they were all dead by now. But I wasn't one hundred percent sure. One day I had been lying in my own filth, and the next I was in the middle of a forest. I was so disoriented I just started walking and eventually ended up in California.

But maybe I had been in California all along.

Gripping the back of my neck, I tried to calm myself down. I wanted to kill that motherfucker for tackling Ivy, but something had stopped me. Well, someone.

I didn't even understand the odd connection I felt to Eli. It wasn't like what I felt toward Ivy, but it was up there. I'd been with men before, and plenty of women, but never had I wanted to protect one so fiercely. Never had I wanted a man to just wrap me in his arms and lock out the world.

As my feet froze in the snow and my body trembled with anxiety, all I wanted was for him to pull me against his warm body and comfort me. If it hadn't been for him, I might not have come back from the claws of my wolf.

After what felt like an hour but was probably a few minutes, Eli cleared his throat. "Maybe we should go inside." He spoke like I was a timid animal that might flee, and I flinched. I was one of the strongest in my pack, and now I was a trembling mess who couldn't even handle going in a helicopter.

"We don't even know these people." My voice was surprisingly steady given the shitstorm going on inside me. I turned my head to look at him and hated the worry I saw in his eyes. "Aren't the two of them enemies? Why would we come here?"

Eli stepped a little closer but didn't touch me, to my dismay. "I don't think Silas will hurt Ivy."

"He tackled her," I snapped, a little harsher than I intended. Eli winced, and I finally turned to face him. "I think we need to be cautious. He might not hurt Ivy, but he might hurt us."

"I agree. With the four of us, we'll be fine. I'm hoping I can get into contact with my sister and Manny. I'm sure there will be a lot of pack members that won't follow Dante's lead. He wasn't well liked." Eli reached out and put a hand on my arm. "Are you okay?"

I shuddered and considered lying to him. "No." My voice cracked.

Eli's face grew even more concerned, and he stepped forward. "Can I hug you?"

"You can always hug me."

He wrapped his arms around me, and I buried my face in the crook of his neck. Why was being comforted by him such an amazing feeling?

I didn't even want to think back to the treehouse when I'd had my hand wrapped around his cock, bringing him to his climax. Being buried inside Ivy and feeling his pleasure had been the biggest high I'd felt in a long time.

"I don't know what happened to you, Xander, but you'll get through it. You have me, Ivy, Cole... Maybe possibly even Silas."

I laughed at that and pulled out of his embrace. "I... I don't know exactly where I was before, and that scares me. One minute I was being tortured and experimented on, and the next, I woke up in the middle of a forest, not knowing how I got there. I'm not even from around here. I'm from Washington."

Eli searched my face and then looked out at the tree line surrounding the property we were on. "I looked in the missing wolf database. I couldn't find anyone named Xander and none of the ten that matched your description were you."

"My name is actually Alexander." I laughed, shaking my head. "I just didn't correct you because I liked the sound of Xander coming from your lips."

"But you said it was Xander." He looked confused.

"My voice wasn't working right. I still want to be called Xander. It's a fresh start." I ran my thumb over his bottom lip. "You wouldn't have found me in your database. I belonged to a small pack, and we didn't use much of the technology available if I'm being honest. I'd like to see the database, though. Maybe." I'd seen a lot of other wolves where I was. Not usually in human form, but occasionally someone would shift. "Maybe I'll recognize some of the missing."

"You've talked about three others." Eli treaded carefully, and I couldn't blame him. I didn't even know my threshold for losing it.

"I think they got most of the pack, all thirty-two of us. I'm not sure if they got the pack we were going to merge with, which was a little smaller." I didn't even want to consider that they had something to do with what happened.

A lot of my memories were muddled. I had been

captured in November, and now it was March. I wasn't sure how long I'd been wandering in the forest, but it couldn't have been that long, could it?

Seeming to sense my spiral, Eli put his arm around me and looked back at the building. "Are you ready to go inside now? That old man meant business."

"Yeah, I think I am."

We walked in the door, and all I could smell was fried breakfast meat. My stomach panged, reminding me I hadn't eaten in a few days, and even before then I'd had very little. The one thing about starvation is that you can't gorge on food or you end up in even more pain.

My stomach was loud enough that Eli chuckled and patted my belly. Normally, I would think that was a childish move, but it brought a smile to my face. It was exactly what I needed.

I followed him into the large room that reminded me of East Arbor's, except this one looked more lived in. There was a large mural of wolves on one wall and windows along the entire upper part of the walls.

The different sitting areas included one that had giant beanbags and another that had three sectionals arranged in a circle around a large coffee table. My mind was in the gutter because I instantly thought about a strip club and how perfect it would be if there was a pole in the middle.

I would be down to watch Ivy climb up there and strip for us... her mates, no one else.

I caught her staring at me from across the room where she sat at a large table that looked like it was made of one solid piece of wood. She gave me an award-winning smile that lit up her entire face and made me forget for a second that I'd just been through hell and back.

She'd been through hell too, and it was nice to see her smile. I tamped down a growl that threatened to escape at the thought of Dante throwing her into the cold river. I wasn't an expert on how rivers worked, but the water was probably freezing. How she'd survived and recovered so quickly was a mystery.

But then again, she had healed Cole, which was something we needed to keep quiet for as long as possible. If word got out that she could heal, I didn't know how other wolves would respond. I would have thought it would be a good thing, but they would probably take advantage of her skill and wonder how the hell she had it to begin with.

If *they* got ahold of her, who knew how far they'd go to find out her secrets and abilities.

I stopped abruptly and shut my eyes. Dammit. I'd been doing so well.

Eli put his hand on the small of my back, and I took a deep breath and opened my eyes. "Sorry, sometimes it's just random moments."

"You don't have to apologize."

I let him guide me to the table, and I sat down next to Ivy. He sat next to me, and Ivy turned toward me and leaned forward slightly so she could see Eli too.

"While you two were outside, we decided to eat, shower, sleep, and then come up with a plan." She examined me closely. "If you want in on the plan."

"I do." I put my arm across the back of her chair and ran my fingers along the ends of her hair. "Don't worry about me."

She bit her lip and put her hand on my thigh. "I just... I know I barely know you... any of you really, but I don't want to see you in pain. Physical or psychological."

The old man from outside sat down across from me and scowled at Ivy. She squeezed my thigh and gave him a smile. Would it be so wrong if I jumped over the table and knocked the old man over?

"From what I hear, you've been stirring up quite a bit of trouble, young lady."

Ivy smiled even wider, and I knew it was to cover her true feelings. "Your grandson has actually caused all the trouble, sir."

The man howled with laughter and his hand smacked down on the table as a cough shook his body. Once the cough had passed, he cleared his throat. "Why are you really here?" His question held an underlying threat to it, and I sat up straighter, ready to pounce.

"I'm here because Silas is my mate, and he's going to help us."

"That's rubbish. There's no such thing as mates!" He acted like he was scandalized, which was curious considering his son had reportedly killed the former alpha.

"Pops, is there a problem?" Silas came through the swinging door leading to the kitchen, holding two big platters filled with food. "Let's put our differences aside until after we eat."

Cole was behind him, a scowl on his face. I was curious about what had transpired in the kitchen. No one had gotten stabbed at least. I had a feeling they were going to have it out before too long, and I wanted a front-row seat. In fact, they should have broadcast it on Pay-Per-View. I'd have paid sixty dollars to see it.

Do I even have sixty dollars?

There were so many things I needed to take care of: logging into my bank account, checking on bills, figuring out if anyone from my pack was still alive.

I narrowed my eyes as Silas put two trays of food in the center of the long table and sat in front of Ivy. Cole had shared with me why the two packs weren't one anymore, and it left me with a sour taste in my mouth.

Killing an alpha was inconceivable. Even in a fight for the alpha position, shifters didn't kill each other. If it was true, Silas's father deserved to die a very painful death, much like Dante was going to as soon as we recuperated.

I couldn't wait to see Dante squeal like a pup and beg for forgiveness. I wasn't one for torture, but something about the entire situation made me want blood, and lots of it.

It was always possible Cole would have mercy and banish him or lock him in the basement, but if he didn't take care of him, I would. Deceiving the alpha and his significant other didn't sit right with me at all.

"I'm so hungry I could eat a horse." Eli licked his lips at the food laid out in front of us.

The spread was impressive with bacon, sausage, eggs, and toast. A woman was the last to come from the kitchen with a giant bowl of cut fruit. She sat down next to Silas, looked at Ivy, then shifted her chair a few inches away from his.

Interesting.

"Dig in." Silas rubbed his hands together, and everyone began serving themselves.

Everyone except me and Eli. The food looked and smelled delicious, but I didn't know if I should trust that these people didn't poison it.

"We don't follow that omega bullshit here." Silas looked at Eli. "So fill up your plate or I'll start making you go first."

Cole slammed his fork down on the table. "Don't tell my omega what to fucking do."

"You're in my den now, I'll tell him and your betas what to fucking do if I want. Oh, wait... your betas deceived you." Silas took a bite of bacon with a smug look on his face.

Cole stood and Ivy clutched his arm, yanking him back down before he could lunge across the table. I was a little disappointed because that would have been fun to watch.

"Both of you need to stop." Ivy handed the bowl of fruit to me. "It's like I'm herding cats."

Silas's grandfather coughed on a piece of food. "Are you just going to let her insult you like that?" He scowled at Silas, his face seeming to be in a permanent frown.

Ivy didn't even flinch at his remark. If anything, it spurred her on, all pleasantries put aside. "Maybe I should start calling him kitten since he calls me bunny."

She stabbed a piece of melon and brought it to her lips. "Or I could call him pussy."

"Puss would suit him well." Cole chuckled, and the tension was almost visible across the table where Silas and his grandfather were.

Eli made a plate for himself before looking over at my still empty plate. "Do you want my plate? I'll make myself another."

"No. There's no guarantee it's not poisoned."

Instead of saying anything, Silas dropped his half-eaten piece of toast onto his plate and slid it across to me. I stared at it and then back up at him as he took my empty plate and filled it up.

I waited until everyone else resumed eating before I took a bite of the half-eaten toast. It was a ridiculous fear, but I couldn't stop myself from worrying something was wrong with it. It's funny how you can be aware of your own anxiety, but be helpless against it.

There had been instances when I trusted the food I was given only to regret it. Unless I was making it myself, there was no guarantee it was safe, and I couldn't take that risk again. Not when there was so much on the line.

A man at the end of the table took a big bite of eggs and frowned at me, picking at my own with a fork. "If we wanted to poison you, we wouldn't be eating it ourselves."

"Or did you take the antidote in the kitchen and are just waiting for us to pass out so you can lock us away?" Before I was taken, I was an avid movie watcher, which made everything ten times worse. Life really could be as fucked up as in the movies.

Silas laughed. "Do you really think I would poison Ivy?"

Stranger things have happened, but I shook my head and picked up a piece of sausage, nibbling on the end of it. After the flavor hit my tongue, I was tempted to inhale it and the rest of them on the platter in the center of the table.

It was quiet as we ate, everyone seeming to be in their own head about recent events.

Once we finished eating, Ivy stood, putting her napkin on her plate. "Thank you for letting us stay here. I know it's a little hard to have someone you don't know come into your home, but hopefully we won't be in the way." Her eyes landed on Silas. "And I hope you don't mind us taking your room, unless you have another room here that has an attached bathroom and a large bed."

Silas's jaw ticked, and he looked at Ivy with something akin to a challenge. I wasn't about to tell him it was a losing battle. I hadn't seen much of Ivy in action, but I could already tell she was a force to be reckoned with.

"And where am I going to sleep?" He crossed his arms over his chest.

"That's not my problem. You have plenty of places out here." She looked around the room, her eyes landing on the beanbags. "There are even some human-sized cat beds over there just for you."

Cole snorted, and she shot him a look. He held up his hands in mock surrender. "Hey, it was funny."

After getting clean towels and fresh sheets, we followed Ivy up the metal stairs that led to a room that was all by itself. The building was some kind of old factory or warehouse, and the room probably used to be an office.

She opened the door, and we filed inside, shutting and locking the door behind us.

Cole groaned and rubbed his hands over his face. "I really don't know if staying is a good idea."

"Then what else do you recommend? You know as soon as Dante can't find us he's going to look in Arbor Falls. He knows where I live, doesn't he?" Ivy walked over to the bed and started stripping off the sheets with Eli.

"Dante knows. We can always go somewhere else; you forget I have money. Although it might be a bit tricky to get it without my ID or card." Cole was sauntering around the room, looking at the posters of motorcycles and pictures on the dresser. I wouldn't have been surprised if he started going through the drawers. "He actually *lives* here?"

"It appears so." I stayed near the door, not liking that there were no windows besides the skylight in the ceiling. Technically, it was a window, but it didn't open, and we couldn't climb through it. What if there was a fire? What if an enemy came and blocked our exit?

"We need backup, but I'm not sure if I trust Silas's pack." Cole picked up an empty picture frame, examined it, then set it down.

Eli changed the pillowcases while Ivy picked up the blankets and sniffed them, wincing and putting them down. "Smells like a wet dog. Probably from me."

She came to stand in front of me and put her hand on my chest. "What do you think, Xander?"

"I think... I'm not going to be able to sleep in this room." I knew that wasn't what she was asking, she was asking for my opinion on Silas. It should have been pretty clear what my opinion on him was, given I attacked his ass outside.

The walls suddenly felt like they were closing in on me and my breath caught in my lungs, making it hard to breathe.

"Because you can smell him?" Her brows pinched together, and she reached for my hand as I reached for the doorknob. "Maybe there are some other spare rooms we can sleep in."

"I need air." I shrugged off her hand, as much as it pained me, and stepped out, shutting the door behind me.

The last thing I wanted her to see was how broken I was.

CHAPTER TEN

Ivy

Staring at the closed door, tears welled in my eyes. I wanted to go after Xander, but I also got the feeling he needed a little space to breathe. It was a lot to handle going from just being around us to being around so many other people and being the center of attention. Not to mention everything he had gone through since he came to us.

Eli went to move past me, and I put my hand on his chest to stop him. "I think he needs a little space right now. I know your instinct is to go after him, but he said he needs air."

Eli went back to the bed, sitting down with a heavy sigh. "The things he told me outside..." He rubbed his hand over his face. "I don't even want to imagine what happened to him."

Cole cleared his throat and took a towel from the stack I'd set on a chair in the corner. "Do we know where he came from?"

"Washington. He doesn't know how he got here." Eli laid back on the bed and looked up at the skylight. "You two can take a shower first. I'm going to go find Silas and see if I can use a laptop or phone to get in touch with Sara. Maybe I'll do a little digging to see if there are any packs that haven't been active."

"We would know if a pack just up and disappeared. Wouldn't we?" Cole threw a towel at me, and I barely caught it before it fell.

Silas's housekeeping could sure use some work. The floor looked like it hadn't been vacuumed in months, and there was a thin layer of dust on every surface. There were still clothes exploding from the dresser too.

It must have been driving Cole nuts.

"Not necessarily. From the little he said, it sounded like they are very traditional and cut off from most of our technology. Maybe they're just one of those smaller packs that broke off from a larger pack and like to keep things old school. But if something happens to one of those packs, no one will know." Eli pinched the bridge of his nose and shook his head. "I guess it's another thing I'll need to bring up at the next technology meeting. Now that we have the missing wolf search up and running, we should find a way to keep tabs on the packs that don't want tabs kept on them."

"Is it safe to have all that stuff on the internet?" I started stripping out of my clothes and both of them had their eyes glued to me. "I mean, if the wrong person came across the information..."

"There's nothing on that system or the dating app that would pinpoint that we are anything but humans. And besides, they're hidden on special servers behind firewalls and passwords. Even if someone got through all of those things, they would never know what it was for. They might think we're some kind of commune or secret society, but that's it." Eli sat up and rubbed his bottom lip, his eyes locked on my tits. "You stripping down like this is really working for me."

I winked and put my pile of clothes on the bed.

"Go take a shower." Cole kissed my temple and yawned. "We need to get some rest so we can think clearly. It's been a long few days."

I snorted. "More like a long week." What day was it even? I really had no sense of time anymore.

When I came out of the bathroom after my shower, Cole was passed out on the bed and Eli was sitting against the headboard, typing on a laptop. There was a comfortable silence in the room besides the faint clicking of the laptop keys.

As tempting as curling up next to Cole was, I needed to check on Xander, and if Silas was around, I wanted to ask him about the picture again.

Pulling my hair back into a ponytail, I secured it with a hair tie I'd found in the bathroom. I was glad Silas had a few lying on the counter to tie back his shoulder length hair. It almost seemed pointless to wear my hair up. If I shifted, anything securing it would be lost forever unless someone went around collecting hair ties and bobby pins.

"I'm going to go see if I can find Xander," I whispered, leaning over and giving Eli a quick kiss.

"He's downstairs on a beanbag chair. I asked Silas if there are any spare rooms, and he said there aren't." He glanced at me briefly and then went back to typing on the computer. "I tapped into your phone. It's been blowing up, so I sent everyone messages saying that you're fine and would call them later. I also emailed your work and told them you'd be out another few weeks."

I should have been mad that he could get into my phone, but I had nothing to hide. I needed to contact quite a few people as soon as I had time. I also wasn't so silent on social media. Hopefully people thought I was just taking a break and didn't send reinforcements to check on me.

"Any word from Sara?"

He shut his eyes. "I know it seems stupid, but I'm kind of scared to look to see if she sent me any messages. What if she didn't get away?"

I put my hand on his outstretched leg and squeezed it reassuringly. "I'm sure she did. Just look. She's probably worried sick about us. I'm sure Cole would like to know if Manny is okay too."

"You're probably right. You should go check on Xander."

I nodded and stood, looking at Cole sleeping peacefully on the bed next to Eli, I still couldn't believe I had four mates.

After shutting the door gently, I went down the stairs and headed for the area with the beanbags. No one else was in the room, so it was quiet enough to get some rest. It felt weird being in such a large room with nothing going on.

Xander was in the middle of a big blue beanbag, staring at the ceiling. There was enough room for a few people, so I wiggled my way next to him, and he wrapped an arm around me.

"Are you all right?" I laid my head on his chest and snuggled up against him.

We hadn't really had time to get to know each other, and I was curious what his life was like before he was taken. Would he even want to share that with me, or would it be too painful?

"I can't be in a room that has no other exits. This room is fine, except people keep passing through every time I try to shut my eyes and go to sleep." He began twirling the hair in my ponytail. "Sometimes I wonder if this is all a dream and if I'm going to wake up and still be locked in the same cage."

Tears welled behind my eyes. "A cage like in Cole's basement?"

"No. One that's meant for dogs." His fingers brushed along my hair over and over again, lightly touching my back and sending a shiver down my spine to pool in my belly. "Their goal was to mistreat us enough that we'd shift to our human form so they could torture us and get information from us."

"Who's they?"

He was quiet, and I began wondering if he'd fallen

asleep. I turned my head and rested my chin on his chest, staring up at him. He looked back at me with glassy eyes before blinking several times. "I don't know who they were."

His face held a boyish charm to it, with eyes that pierced my soul. There was so much pain and torment in them. I just wanted to hold on to him forever and never let him go. Who would do such a thing to somebody? Even to a wolf?

Was it the government? A rival pack? Some rogue group of humans that wanted to use wolves for their own bidding?

The uncertainty of it all made me nervous. Once we figured out the Dante situation, we needed to figure out what had happened to Xander and his pack. Surely with a pack as large as ours, we'd be able to handle a group of sadistic torturers.

"Do you two need a room?" Silas had come from nowhere and stood over us. "I mean, I'm down to watch, but I really don't want the rest of my pack seeing."

I rolled my eyes and lifted my head to narrow my eyes at Silas. "Must you be so crass?"

"It was just a joke, bunny." He ran his hand over his beard, straightening the blonde strands that had gotten out of place.

"Do you have any rooms with a window or another door to the outside? I know you have that storage room with all the boxes, but that's not really a good place to sleep." He tensed a bit, and I sat up, cocking my head to the side. "What's in the boxes, Silas?"

"Supplies." He cleared his throat and looked across the room to a dimly lit hallway. "We have a bunk room with four beds, and it has a window." Silas looked back at me and then grinned. "That's the only room left, and I'm in desperate need of a nap. Looks like we'll be roomies since you commandeered my room."

I pushed myself off the beanbag and stood in front of him. "You're not sleeping in the room with us. You can sleep out here."

"So it's going to be like that, huh?" He cocked a brow. "How long was it until they all got to sleep in your bed?"

I scoffed. "That's none of your damn business. Did you forget that you and Cole are enemies? Or that your two betas practically killed us? Were you even aware that crash caused me to shift for the first time?"

He backed up a step and looked me up and down in disbelief. "But... How old are you?"

"I just turned twenty-six that night. Thanks for ruining my birthday, by the way. I'll let you make it up to me by getting me a chocolate cake." I put my hand out to help Xander up. "Now, if you'll excuse us, we need a nap."

Silas showed us to the room and a dormitory set of bathrooms. He left us standing in the hall, and my shoulders relaxed.

"Are you going to be okay if I take a shower?" Xander examined the room and then came back out again. "I'll be quick."

"I can handle myself." I kissed his cheek and gave him a smile. "Go shower and then we can take a nap."

We parted ways, and I went into the room and sat on the bottom of one of the bunk beds. The beds were all twin-sized, but that just meant me and Xander could cuddle up next to each other.

It reminded me a lot of the dorms in college where you shared a room but shared the bathroom with the entire floor. It wasn't exactly homey. Even Silas's room was cold and unwelcoming with the lack of windows and gray walls.

I was just about to lie down and get comfortable when the door opened, and Silas walked in. My stomach fluttered as he carried in a plate with a piece of cake and a lit candle on the top.

"Does this suffice as an apology?" He held the plate in front of me, and my mouth watered as the smell of rich chocolate invaded my senses.

It was the most decadent looking piece of chocolate cake I'd ever seen, and I'd seen a lot. The sponge was fluffy, and the chocolate frosting had a glossy sheen to it.

"Depends on if its edible." It was awfully suspicious that he just had a slice of cake and birthday candles lying around.

He grinned and brought the plate closer. "Happy belated birthday, bunny. Make a wish."

I shut my eyes and wished that things would settle down so I could really enjoy this new life and get back to normal. I opened my eyes and blew out the candle.

"What did you wish for?"

"I wished that you would stop calling me bunny."

"Since you said it out loud, it won't come true."

We both laughed and our eyes met. I felt the pull toward him, but that didn't mean I had to act on it. He still had to prove to me he wouldn't hurt us.

Yet, I was in a room alone with him.

"You just had a chocolate cake like this sitting around?" I wouldn't have been shocked if there was magic involved. If there were mermaid-like creatures and wolves, what else was there?

I grabbed the plate and fork from him and took a bite of the most delicious cake I'd ever had. "Shit, this is good. Did you make this?"

Damn. Eli could cook and so could Cole. I had no clue about Xander, but if Silas was a baker? I was a goner.

Silas laughed and looked at the bed next to me and then at the opposite bunk. I saw the wheels spinning in his head, and he finally sat down across from me on the other bed.

"Carly likes to bake. There's always cakes, pies, cookies, you name it. I'd love to say that I made it, but then you'd expect me to always bake like that. If you ever want me to bake you something, I can make you some weed brownies. That's about it. And usually I burn them nine times out of ten."

"Weed brownies?" I licked the back of the fork, Silas's eyes glued to the movement. "There isn't weed in this cake, is there?"

"You got something against weed?" He put his hands behind him and leaned back, his arms and chest stretching his dark gray t-shirt across his muscles. It was surprising he had no tattoos, at least not on his upper half.

"Doesn't it fuck wolf shifters up?" I ate one last bite of the cake before setting it on a small side table at the end of the bed. Maybe Xander would want some.

"It's definitely more potent for us. It's fun. You should try it sometime." He pushed off the bed and came across the room the short distance.

I looked up at him as he leaned one of his forearms on the top bunk and brought his hand toward my face. I shuddered as he wiped across my bottom lip and brought his thumb to his mouth, licking the small bit of chocolate frosting from it.

"Try it?" I spluttered before clearing my throat. "I tried some back in college and about burned my lungs out." I rubbed my chest at the memory.

He was still standing over me but didn't touch me again. I kept my eyes on his because if I looked down, the button on his jeans would be right at eye-level.

"Did you like the cake?" His eyes were hooded, and it didn't take a rocket scientist to know he was thinking about eating the cake between my legs.

"It was all right." *Don't look down.* "So… are we going to talk about the picture?"

"What about it? That you think he's your father? I'm not so sure of that, Ivy." I didn't like that he didn't call me by my nickname, which was disturbing since I thought it was cheesy. "I was young when he died, but I never saw him with a woman, or heard him talking about a woman. It's not like wolf shifters can hide their relationships either. We were the only pack for hundreds of miles."

"You were a child."

"I think we would have noticed a pregnant wolf around." He pushed off the bunk and his eyes widened. "You said you just turned twenty-six. When's your birthday?"

"March thirteenth is what's on my birth certificate. But the paperwork says they found me the morning of the fourteenth. Why?"

"Fuck!" He began pacing the room, running his hands repeatedly through his hair and then gripping the back of his neck.

"What is it?" I stood without thinking and smashed my head into the top bunk. "Motherfucker!"

Silas rushed to me and examined my head before he pulled me against him, wrapping his arms around me. "Shit, bunny. My dad found the alpha dead on the fourteenth of March, twenty-six years ago."

CHAPTER ELEVEN

Ivy

My body went numb, and I slumped against Silas, who tightened his hold on me and walked me toward the bed. We sat down, and he touched my cheek with the tips of his fingers.

"Talk to me. Are you okay?" His eyes told me he was truly concerned. "Ivy?"

I blinked and shook my head.

How could I be okay when it seemed likely that my birth and the alpha's death were connected to each other? "So who's my mother then? Do you think she killed him?"

"Baron was in love with being an alpha, and everyone respected him. It makes no sense that someone would kill him unless they had something to gain." He shook his head. "What would your birth mother gain?"

"Freedom?" If no one knew he got a woman pregnant, maybe he was hiding her away somewhere against her will, or maybe I read too much fiction. "Your father and Cole's father accused each other." I scooted back on the bed and leaned up against the wall. "I think your dad knew about me."

Silas's face fell and his frown deepened. It wasn't a good look on him. I definitely preferred his smile. Something about his frown made him seem harsh, like he'd rip my heart out of my chest and eat it.

"Why do you think that?"

"He paid to have me adopted far away from here." I put my hand on my forehead. I felt cold, like I was coming down with something. Something called shock.

A mixture of emotions passed over Silas's face. First shock and then anger. He stood and glared down at me. "That's impossible. He wouldn't do that."

"Unless there's another pack member that's a biker with blonde hair, green eyes, and a scar on his face."

"Where did you get this information?" Silas began pacing, his arms crossed over his chest.

"The social worker that handled the adoption. Your father paid him half a million dollars. So, please, continue telling me how your father didn't know."

He stopped in his tracks and turned toward me. "My family has never had that kind of money."

"Well, he got the money somehow. Unless the social worker was lying, but what would be the point of that?"

The social worker risked a lot by telling me about the money, so it was doubtful it was a lie. "Where's your father, Silas?"

"I don't know where he is." His voice was strained.

"I find that hard to believe. He just up and left?" I wondered if he was in the missing wolf database. I'd have to have Eli look.

"As soon as I was ready to become alpha, which was questionable, he just left. I haven't heard from him since. I don't-"

The door opened and Xander came in, his brown hair still wet from his shower and dripping onto the shoulders of his t-shirt.

He looked from me, to Silas, and back to me again. "What's going on here?" He strode into the room, stopping in front of Silas. "Should you even be in here alone with her?"

"Xander, he's fine." I laid down on the bed, resting my head on a fluffy pillow and pulling a blanket over me. "Let's nap and figure everything out later."

I wanted to figure everything out, but also knew getting to the bottom of my origins might take some expert level sleuthing. Was it possible my mother wasn't a wolf? That could explain why my wolf looked different and the delay in shifting for the first time.

Xander moved toward the bed and then turned to look at Silas. "Is there a reason you're still here?"

"I'm taking a nap too. Your arrival this morning woke me up well before I was ready." He went to the door and shut it firmly, flicking the lock.

Silas toed off his boots while pulling his shirt off by

the back of the neck. Men just didn't know what that action did to women. Or maybe they did, and that's why they did it. My eyes were glued to him. Being a wolf sure had some perks, like bodies that would take hours a day in the gym and plates full of spinach to achieve.

"Not sure how I'm going to be able to sleep in here with you. I don't know you." Xander crossed his arms over his chest and didn't move from where he was.

"Well, then I guess you don't take a nap." Silas unbuttoned his jeans and pulled them off. I shut my eyes since he had on nothing underneath. Damn. "You're welcome to sleep in the great room, but I can't guarantee that my pack will be quiet when they come in and see you sleeping. You might even wake up with a Sharpie dick on your face."

Xander grumbled, and the bed shifted as he laid down next to me. I could smell the clean scent of the soap and shampoo he'd used, and I wanted to bury my nose against his skin.

"Is his dick covered yet?" It took every bit of my willpower not to peek.

"He's in the bed now. I'm so sorry you had to see that." Xander laid on his back and put his arm around me as I cuddled up against his side.

"I don't think I'll ever get over what I just saw. I'm scarred for life." I laughed and yawned at the same time.

Silas grumbled under his breath and punched the pillow on the bed a few times before rolling over with his back to us. He had not one tattoo.

Xander must have been fine with Silas after all, because within a few minutes, he was passed out, and I followed soon after.

~

SOMETHING warm and wet on my stomach woke me. My hand moved to brush it off, but ran right into a head. *What the hell is Xander doing?*

Realization dawned on me and my thighs instantly squeezed together as a shock of desire went directly between my legs. I couldn't see him because he was under the blanket, but I could feel him.

Open-mouthed kisses traveled up my stomach and his hand pushed up my shirt. I was still covered, but I couldn't help but look over at Silas's bed to make sure he was sleeping.

He wasn't.

Cocking a brow, he rolled onto his side and pushed the sheet he had over himself down to his waist, exposing his broad chest and tapered waist. I bit my lip as Xander latched onto a nipple, swirling and sucking the sensitive bud.

"*Silas is watching.*" Just the words alone made heat pool in my core.

"*Let him.*" Xander pushed down my pants and his fingers slid over my wet slit. "*Let him see how a real man pleases a woman.*"

A finger slid inside of me and began pumping without hesitation. I swallowed a gasp and my back arched when he added a second finger. He moved down my body and settled between my legs, his warm breath on my thigh.

Silas's hand was resting on his chest, and he swiped his thumb across his nipple, back and forth, circling, a slight pinch, repeat. A moan escaped my lips, and he brought his fingers to his mouth, licking them before returning them to his nipple.

Xander nudged my legs wider and lowered his mouth to my clit. There was nothing that turned me on more than a man between my thighs, and I throbbed as he licked and swirled his tongue.

My orgasm was building and the scene playing out across the room was making it harder to not let go and spiral into a whirlpool of bliss. Silas's hand traveled down his abdomen and under the sheet. I wanted to protest him not showing himself.

Xander's tongue sliding inside me alongside his fingers had me clenching my legs around his head and I was done for. My pussy clenched around him as he played my clit like he was performing a violin concerto at the Metropolitan Opera House. I cried out and kept my eyes on Silas as he pumped his cock under the sheet, his chest heaving as he watched me come undone as another man brought me to release.

Xander moved back up the bed, resting his forearms next to my head. He buried his cock inside of me, nuzzling my neck. "Fuck, you feel so good."

"Yes, oh God, Xander." I wrapped my legs around him and rolled my hips up to meet each thrust.

"Harder," Silas rasped from across the room.

Xander's head lifted from the crook of my neck and perused Silas's body. "Move the sheet."

Silas grunted and his jaw ticked. I could tell he was mulling it over when Xander stopped, a challenge in his eyes. They stared each other down for a good minute, a war of wills and my pussy their casualty.

"Fuck me, please." I tried bucking my hips, but the way he was lying on me left me immobile.

"Not until we get a show like we're giving him." A slow grin formed on Xander's lips, and he swiveled his hips to tease me, his pelvis rubbing against my clit.

"You want a show?" Silas rasped, the sound of a man barely holding it together.

He stood, the sheet falling to the floor, fisting his cock with an iron grip. A bead of pre-cum sat at the tip and he swiped his thumb across it, moving it over his shaft.

I thought the treehouse—both times—was the hottest thing ever, but this was cataclysmic, solar implosion level hot.

Xander began moving again in quick, hard thrusts that left me breathless. He shrugged the blanket off us, and Silas worked his cock harder and faster.

"Kiss me," I barely managed to get out. I grabbed Xander by the back of the neck and pulled him to me, sealing our lips together in a hard kiss that would leave our lips red and swollen.

Silas cursed, his cum spilling onto his hand at the same time Xander came inside me. My orgasm wasn't long after, milking Xander for every drop.

Still panting, I covered my eyes with my forearm. These men were going to be the death of me.

~

I WOKE UP WITH A START, my heart pounding in my chest and my fangs scraping against my lower lip. Damn dreams about deer. Until I had shifted, I never remembered my dreams, but now I could remember every detail.

The twitch of the juicy vein in its neck. A flick of its ear. The first drop of its blood.

I slid out of bed from under Xander's arm and quickly made my way to the door. I was foolish to think that my days of popping a fang boner over deer were over. How long ago had it last happened? The days were all blurring together, and it felt like it had been way longer than it had.

I was barely out the door when Silas took my hand. "Are you okay?" he whispered.

I led him out of the room and pointed to my mouth. His jaw opened in surprise, and I headed toward the back door of the building. Carly and a few others were in the room, but they didn't pay us any attention, even though we were both naked.

As soon as we were out the door, Silas took my hand again and pulled me to a stop. "What are you doing? Just breathe deeply and they should go away. You're not going out there alone."

"I can do what I want." I pulled my hand away and began walking across the space toward the forest.

The snow had almost already melted, and if I had to guess, the temperature was around seventy degrees. It amazed me how one second there was practically a blizzard and the next it was like spring was upon us. I needed to get back to work at Northern Alliance.

The helicopter sat in the middle of the grass, looking completely out of place and an even bigger reminder of what had been taken away from me so abruptly.

I didn't know where I was going, and I didn't know what I was going to do, I just knew I needed to run. And maybe find a deer.

Before I could even think twice, I shifted to my wolf. I looked behind me to find Silas jogging toward me, a glint in his eye. If I wasn't so focused on food, I'd have taken a moment to stare.

I lifted my nose to the sky and sniffed. It smelled slightly different from Cole's territory. I didn't know how I knew, but I could smell the unique mixture of wolves. Maybe I needed to work on remembering scents.

The faint hint of a deer hit my nose, and I took off running. I heard Silas shift behind me and his chuffs as he ran. I felt so alive running through the forest with my mate at my heels.

There were still some patches of snow, but most had melted, leaving the ground damp and muddy in some places. Sun filtered through the trees, and I tilted my face up as I ran, trying to capture some warmth. I bet a sun bath would feel divine, but after a snack.

I was ravenous, and I knew the only way to satisfy

my belly and my beast was with what I craved. My mind and heart, however, were heavy at the thought of killing another deer. What the heck was wrong with me? I was at war with myself, and the animalistic side won.

I slowed as the scent got stronger and stronger. I could see it now, but it couldn't see me. Even if it ran, I would chase after it and take it down. It had to be three times my size, with antlers and a beautiful tawny color.

I ran at a sprint. The buck, realizing I was coming, turned to begin its escape. It was fast, but I was faster.

My legs burned with exertion, my breaths coming out steadily as I tried to control my breathing. With one giant leap, I was on top of him, my fangs ripping into his neck.

He fell, nearly squashing me underneath him, but I wiggled out of the way just in time, not letting go of my hold on his neck until he stopped moving.

Taking them down was always the worst part. But then it was over, and my mind was on one thing: food.

I was just starting to enjoy my meal when Silas came up beside me and tried sticking his nose in my dinner. I bared my teeth and delivered a warning growl.

He growled right back, and I lost it. I surged forward, moving him away from my precious, snapping my teeth at him. He snapped back at me, and we circled each other, a dance of two beasts vying for dominance.

Our bodies collided, tangling together. He wasn't biting me, only giving me hard nudges with his muzzle, but my teeth scraped against his legs a few times as we tumbled on the forest floor.

With a hard butt of my head to his abdomen, he fell to the ground, staying there and looking up at me. I longed to take his throat, opening my jaw but not biting down. His snarls filled my ears as he fought against the urge to give up his dominance.

After what felt like years, he fell silent, but he didn't roll over. I had the feeling he would never roll over for me.

I released him and backed up. *"Why did you follow me?"*

I don't know why I spoke to him that way, but something innate told me we had a connection now. What that meant exactly, I was just going to ignore. For now.

"I wanted to make sure you were safe. What the hell is happening right now? How did you do that?" He was still on the ground, staring up at me with wolf eyes that were not unlike Eli's and Cole's, but a lighter shade of amber.

"I have no idea. For a while, both Cole and I had connections to Eli. I still do... with all three of them, but I don't know if Cole can talk to Eli anymore." I swiveled my head and looked back at the deer. *"Dammit. I don't like killing deer, but I can't stop myself."*

Silas finally got to his feet and carefully walked over to assess the dead animal. *"He's a big one. I'm surprised you took him down."*

We stared down at Bambi's father, and a tear dripped down my face. Silas came closer to me and nuzzled his head against my shoulder. *"Don't worry about it. I'll have Bone come out here and grab him for dinner. Just think of them like cows of the forest."*

"Cows of the forest?" I snorted and wondered what it looked like when a wolf smiled. I needed to find a mirror and check my wolf out.

"Like tuna is the chicken of the sea." Silas sniffed the air and started walking farther into the forest. *"Are you coming?"*

"The den is back the other way. Where are you going?" I took a few steps after him, but hesitated.

"I want to show you something." He took off like a bullet, and I was left with no other choice but to follow him or go back alone.

My curiosity piqued, so I ran after him, easily catching up and matching our strides as we ran through the forest.

After a few minutes, we exited the trees into a clearing, a large cabin standing before us. It had been neglected for what looked like several years. There were vines and foliage growing up the sides of it, and dead leaves and branches on the roof.

If I hadn't watched so many horror movies about cabins in the woods, I would have been all for a little adventure. *"What is this place?"*

"It's my family home." He shifted back and walked toward the porch steps. "I haven't been here in a while, but now that you're around, maybe I'll fix it back up again."

I followed him, not shifting back yet, and sniffed the air cautiously. It smelled safe, but what did I know?

"Are you going to shift so I can show you inside?" Silas turned and looked at me.

"No. I've seen how this horror movie plays out."

In a flash, Silas shifted back to his wolf and was right in front of me. He started licking at my muzzle, and I was so shocked that I just stood there, processing that he was kissing me, and I was letting him.

CHAPTER TWELVE

Silas

This woman had my wolf at her feet and wanting to roll over. He wanted nothing more than to please her, which went strictly against the alpha side of me. If any other would have come at me like she had, they would have been put in their place.

When she told me no, I shifted quicker than I ever had. My intention was to give her a nip to the hindquarters and remind her I was the alpha in this territory, but instead, I gave her muzzle a good lick.

I'd never been so bold with another female wolf before. In fact, I don't think I'd ever made a move on a woman while she was in her wolf form. At least from what I could remember.

I was just about to give her face a little nibble when she snapped at me, nearly taking off my tongue.

Jesus, she was feisty, but I liked it. I liked it a lot.

"So, this is how it's going to be?" I backed up a few steps to make sure she didn't take off the end of my nose. A nose scar wasn't an attractive look. *"Can't I get to know my mate more?"*

"As a wolf?" Her teeth were still showing, and her ears went back a little. *"You kissed me! What's next? Are you going to mount me like a dog?"*

I let out a yip. *"If that's what you want, it can be arranged."*

She chuffed. *"Why are we here?"*

"I want to show you my home... your home." I got an uneasy feeling in my belly, like she was about to turn and give me her back. *"Is this how you were with the other three, too?"*

"I don't know you and what I do know doesn't work in your favor." Her words stung, and I wanted to tuck my tail between my legs but dug deep to stop it from happening.

"You don't know them hardly either." I sniffed the air and groaned. *"Great. Just perfect."*

Cole came tramping out of the woods, and his hair bristled when he saw me and Ivy standing close together.

"The two packs don't get along. What am I supposed to do with that? I don't want to play mediator."

"What if I would've found you first? Because then they'd be the enemies and not me." She cocked her head to the side in consideration. She knew I was right.

Cole walked right between us, turning so our muzzles were almost touching. He growled, but I didn't back up, letting out my own. I knew exactly what he was saying without actually hearing his words.

He was trying to stake his claim on her, but I wasn't about to let him. For the second time, I found myself in a fight for dominance. We lunged at each other, his teeth snapping and our anger growing louder and louder. It was a long time coming.

We rolled around on the ground, getting mud all over ourselves. For Cole having been shot and poisoned not too long ago, his strength seemed to be perfectly fine. Had it all been an act to infiltrate my pack and take over?

He rammed into me from the side and sent me flying, my head hitting the ground and a jolt of pain running through the side of my skull.

I pulled myself to my feet and stumbled a bit. My head felt fuzzy, and a trickle of something ran down the side of it. The copper scent of blood permeated my nose, and I felt like vomiting.

"Stop it!" Ivy's voice pierced my brain, and I realized she was standing over me in her human form. "Can't you men just get along? You fight and bicker more than two teenage girls."

I flopped down onto the ground and whimpered like a newborn pup. Damn, my head hurt. Had I cracked my skull wide open? I wasn't sure, but it felt like it.

Ivy's hands went to my head, pulling the fur away from the wound and examining it. "This is a pretty nasty gash. It's probably going to need stitches or staples or whatever it is you guys use."

"What the hell did he hit his head on?" Cole stood next to her and looked past me to where I had originally fallen. "Damn, that's a pretty jagged rock."

Cursing under his breath, he scooped me up and carried me toward the house. "There should be a key under that statue of a wolf."

"You really need a key out here?" She pushed the bronzed wolf up to grab the key underneath.

"Wolves can be criminals too."

While they were discussing wolves breaking into each other's houses, my vision was growing blurrier by the second. Damn, I'd really done a number on myself. It was all Cole's fault, too. If he would have just let us be, we would never have gotten in a fight. I looked up at him with narrowed eyes that made my head hurt even worse.

"Don't give me that look." Cole rolled his eyes. "You're just as much to blame for this as I am. What did you think was going to happen when you came out here alone with her?"

Well, I thought I'd get to spend some one-on-one time with my mate. This might not have been *The Bachelorette*, but I fully intended on getting my rose.

Ivy opened the door and stepped inside the house. The smell of dust filled my nose, and I sneezed. It had been too long since I'd been out there. It was a really nice house too, it just got lonely out in the middle of the woods with no one else around.

Cole carried me into the kitchen and put me on the kitchen table. A towel was pressed to my head and fingers stroked along my spine. Warmness and tingles spread across my entire body.

"You're healing him," Cole whispered.

"I am not." There was a moment of silence, and Ivy let out a strained laugh. "Okay, I guess I am."

The head wound must have been too much for my brain, and I was hallucinating. My vision popped with color and then nothing mattered anymore as the darkness took me.

~

I WOKE to the sound of what sounded like wood cracking. Rubbing my eyes, I sat up in my bed and looked around my bedroom. What was that?

I heard the sound again and my dad's hushed curse. I scrambled out of bed and rushed across my room, ignoring the pain in my foot when I stepped on a stray building brick and not caring if I kicked over what I was building.

I threw open my door and ran down the hall. My dad was kneeling on the floor where the couch should've been, prying the wooden floorboards up with a crowbar.

"Dad?" I rubbed my eyes again, trying to see more clearly. I padded across the living room and his head turned toward me, a manic look in his eyes. "What's wrong?"

Why was he destroying the floor?

"Go back to bed, son." He went back to prying up the floor.

"What are you doing?" I drew closer, and then I saw what he was after. There were two rusty metal boxes in the floor,

but I didn't know what was inside. "Why are you destroying the floor?"

My dad put down the crowbar and reached down into the hole he had created to grab one of the boxes. He dug in his pocket and pulled out his keys.

"Go to your room," *he bit out, causing the hairs on my arms to stand on end.*

My dad was never so short with me, and tears welled in my eyes. Had I done something wrong?

He put the key in the lock and turned it, opening the lid with a loud squeak. There was a lot of cash inside.

"Whoa... What's that for?"

He didn't answer me and instead picked up a duffel bag that was to the side of him and began throwing the bundled money inside. Had he robbed a bank or maybe won the lotto?

"Go to bed. I'm not going to say it again." *He turned and looked at me then, warning in his eyes and fangs showing.*

I ran to my room, tears streaming down my face.

WE NEVER TALKED about what I'd seen that night. I had even forgotten all about it until Ivy had said my dad had paid off a social worker to make sure she was far from Arbor Falls. I wished I had a way to contact him so I could find out what the fuck he'd done.

Fingers ran across the top of my head and circled around my ear, making me feel like I was floating on a cloud. If I could stay as a wolf forever and have the sensation of fingers running across my head, I would in an instant.

"I don't really know why he doesn't come back here

anymore." I heard Cole in the room, the wooden floors creaking under his steps as he walked around. "There are some photo albums. Maybe we can find some pictures of Baron."

"We need to talk to his grandpa and other older pack members and see what they know." The fingers stroking my head belonged to my bunny. I didn't want her to stop, so I kept my eyes closed. "Why would Silas's dad pay to have me adopted away from here, though?"

"No clue. The only person who would know that answer is probably him and maybe Silas's grandpa. We'll have to talk to him. He was never a very nice man. He scared the shit out of me growing up." I felt the same way as Cole.

My grandpa had this way about him that made me think he would snap my neck in an instant, even though I was his only grandson. He lived nearby, but mostly kept to himself, coming to the den for breakfast and sometimes dinner, but never saying much.

It was surprising he'd said so much at breakfast and actually laughed. But maybe that was something to be more nervous about.

"What about Silas's mom?" Ivy stroked down my snout and between my eyes. Jesus, did she know what she was doing to me? It was taking every piece of my willpower not to roll over and ask for a belly rub.

I didn't do belly rubs.

"She died when he was born, so it was just him and his dad. A lot of the females in the pack, including my mom, helped take care of him, but his dad never remarried as far as I know."

The couch dipped as Cole sat down, his scent wafting over to me. As much as I wanted to bite him in the ass, my wolf had missed his smell. He was like a brother growing up, and when our dads had become enemies, so had we.

I heard the spine of the photo album crack as he opened it and the sound of the laminated pages being turned. They were quiet as they looked through it.

Ivy made a noise of consideration. "I don't look like him unless I'm laughing really hard. What do you think?"

"Nothing obvious. I mean, you definitely have his alpha personality. Maybe you take after your mom. Whoever that may be."

"Maybe... if she was in this pack, someone would have known her or seen her walking around pregnant. How far away is the nearest pack?"

"Tahoe." Tahoe was a few hours away.

"Maybe I was conceived in a night of passion... but that doesn't explain why I was abandoned here and not wherever she was from... or the money. The money is highly suspicious." She paused and then giggled. "Silas was a cute baby."

Happiness welled up in me that my mate thought I was cute, and my damn tail wagged. I stopped it from doing more than one quick hit on the sofa, but still, the damage was done.

"Silas is awake. I was worrying there for a second."

Cole's laugh wasn't fooling me. Fucker had been worried more than just a second.

"No, he's not. He's still passed out. Look at him." She hit a sensitive spot behind my ear and my traitorous tail wagged again.

"His tail just wagged." Damn tail couldn't keep a secret to save its life, and the hand on my head stilled.

"Maybe he was having a wolf dream... like dogs do."

I shifted back, my head face down in her lap, which was covered by only a pillow. She shoved me away, and I sat up, sticking out my bottom lip. "Since you think I'm a dog, can I smell your crotch?"

"Ew." She scrunched her nose in the most adorable way and then a pillow hit me across the face, falling into my lap.

"Hey, what the fuck?"

"Cover yourself, you filthy animal." Cole's voice held a lightness that I hadn't heard from him since we were young.

I threw the pillow back at his head, and Ivy groaned. "Can we not have a pillow fight with me in the middle?" She folded her arms over her breasts. There probably weren't any clothes in the cabin to change into.

"He started it." I knew I sounded like a child, but that was how I felt when it came to Cole. He had been my best friend, my unofficial brother, and then suddenly he wasn't. I didn't think we could repair our relationship to what it once was, not after everything we'd been through, the words we'd exchanged, the fights we'd been in.

"Maybe you two should just start over. Don't continue to make your fathers' mistakes." She stood, turning to face us. "How are we going to work if you're always at each other's throats? I can't have my boyfriends wanting to kill each other."

"I'm your boyfriend?" I sat up a little straighter, and Cole dramatically huffed and rolled his eyes. "Why don't you say how you really feel, Coco?"

"Don't call me that. We're not kids anymore." He stood and wrapped an arm around Ivy's waist. "I worry about your ability to protect our mate."

I cringed. That was the worst thing he could have possibly said. "And what about you? She was thrown into a freezing river without any way to get herself free. What if a human would have found her like that?"

Cole's jaw ticked, and his fingers dug into her waist. "I can't control other people's actions, Si. He blindsided me."

"And that's something that should never happen as the alpha of a large pack." I stood and grabbed the photo album from the couch. "But maybe we were never meant to be alphas."

"What the hell is that supposed to mean?" Cole snatched the album from me and threw it on the coffee table.

"Bunny is an alpha, and she's stronger than us." She gasped, and I grinned at her reaction. "I'm sure if you'd get your head out of your ass for once, you would have already realized it."

"I do not want to be the alpha of anything. Besides, Cole told me women are never strong enough." She moved away from both of us and started to pace. She was already such a natural at being a wolf, not even caring that she was naked as the day she was born. "This is all too much."

Cole ran his hand down his face and then crossed his arms over his chest. "I think he's right."

She stopped and stared at us both, her eyes smoldering and her red hair making her look like the queen she was. "So now what?"

I put my hand on Cole's shoulder and he looked at it with a cocked brow. "Now, we get Cole's pack back and become one."

Emotion overwhelmed me, and I turned away. I wouldn't be alone anymore.

CHAPTER THIRTEEN

Eli

My sister was alive, and it had lifted a huge weight from my shoulders. If something would have happened to her, I didn't know what I would have done.

When we'd lost our mom and she'd been near death herself, I lost myself to my wolf. We had both been close to our mother, and her loss was something I didn't think I'd ever truly get over.

Sara had been the one to pull me out of my spiral into darkness. Our dad had carried her down the stairs and she'd stood on her one leg, supported by crutches, and told me to snap the hell out of it because she needed me.

And she did. She needed me more than she was willing to admit.

I headed downstairs after taking a shower, tired of being locked away up in the room. Cole had taken a long nap while I confirmed reinforcements were coming to help us and made sure our assets weren't compromised. I considered sending a mass email, but wanted to discuss it with Cole first, but he had disappeared when I was in the shower.

Surely out of the three hundred plus members of the pack, most would join with us to take back the pack. We were still human at our core, and what Dante had done was treason. Cole could beat him in a fight, but we now knew Dante didn't fight fair.

The sun was setting, and I smelled the aromas of roasting meat wafting from the kitchen as I walked down the stairs. Looking around the room, I found it was empty besides a lone figure on a beanbag chair watching an action movie.

I smiled to myself and walked across the room to where Xander was. He looked away from the screen for a moment to give me a small smile and then went back to watching his movie.

It shouldn't have ruffled my feathers, but my stomach flopped, and I looked around the room awkwardly. "Can I, uh, join you?"

Jesus, I sounded lame.

I approached the beanbag right next to his, and he reached out and pulled me down next to him.

My heart nearly jumped out of my chest at the sudden change in direction. Not at all because he pulled me close, his hand wrapped around me and resting on my hip.

"I... uh..." I gulped and held myself awkwardly against him, resisting the urge to put my hand on his chest and relax into him.

"You can join me, but only if you're right here next to me." He squeezed my hip and then moved his hand to rub the skin just over the waistband of my pants. "Is that all right with you?"

Was it? I didn't know what was happening. Had I ever fathomed the thought of being intimate with another guy? No. Did I loathe the idea? No.

"What about Ivy?" I pulled my bottom lip between my teeth.

"It's not like I'm asking to suck your dick right now." His eyes didn't leave the television screen. "Lay with me."

My cheeks puffed as I blew out a breath. "What if someone sees us?"

He looked at me. "So? Fuck them if they can't handle seeing two men cuddling and enjoying each other's company. Unless you're the one who can't handle it."

We stared into each other's eyes for a solid minute before I let myself relax against him. I was practically planking against his side, and he wiggled his knee between my legs and took my hand, putting it on his chest.

It felt... comfortable.

Resting my head on his chest, I turned my attention to the movie he was watching. I had no clue what it was, but they were in the middle of a car chase. I preferred reading, but hadn't even had time to do that lately.

I was very aware of Xander's hand as it slid up my side under my shirt, his fingers trailing lightly over my heated skin. Heated because my blood was boiling under his touch.

He clearly had no problems with being with a man, and that made me wonder just how many men he'd been with.

His hand left my skin and disappointment filled me, but it was only to move to my head where his fingers ran through the slicked back strands.

"I can practically hear you thinking," he mumbled.

My scalp tingled with his touch, and I shut my eyes. "I haven't uh... done anything with a guy before."

He grunted, and his fingers went to my ear. I groaned as I fisted his shirt without thinking.

"Well, you're doing a pretty good job."

I opened my mouth to respond when the door opened, and Sara's scent caused me to leap up.

She looked around the room as Bone came from the kitchen wearing an apron that said *I'm the cock in this kitchen* with a picture of a rooster cooking.

"Who the hell are you?"

Sara bypassed him and headed straight for me. We met halfway, wrapping our arms around each other. I hadn't realized how much I'd missed her until that moment, and I felt like crying.

"Can someone tell me what the hell is going on? Silas didn't say others would be showing up." Bone was hemming and hawing about dinner, Carly telling him there would be enough food, regardless.

The back door flew open with a loud clang, Ivy, Cole, and Silas coming in.

"Sara!" I was surprised that Ivy was so animated about seeing my sister again after barely meeting her. Maybe they'd really bonded over her escape from the mall and video games.

"Ivy!" Sara squealed as Ivy picked her up in a bear hug.

"Manny!" Cole had a huge grin on his face and pulled Manny into an awkward hug with lots of back slapping.

It seemed everyone was coming together at once, a cacophony of voices in the once quiet room.

Looking over my shoulder to where Xander and I had been snuggling, I found him missing, the television still playing the movie. I looked around, just catching his back as he went down a hall.

"Now that we have the brains of the pack back, let's get going on contacting our members." Cole gave Sara a hug and then turned to me. "Go get that laptop."

I was going to ignore his playful jab that Sara was the brains. I was just as capable of sending out emails too, but Sara was better at how to word things. Plus, we both knew who in the pack might side with Dante over Cole.

"But Xander..." I looked to the hall he'd disappeared down.

"He said not to bother him." Ivy put her hand on my

arm. "He'll be fine. Just too many people and too much noise."

I sighed and went to get the laptop from upstairs when all I wanted was to make sure he was okay.

~

"I sent the email. Let's hope we picked the right wolves." Cole stretched his arms over his head and then folded them on top of it. We'd been discussing for an hour which pack members were most likely not following Dante's ploy and had a working dinner.

"You might just have to take him out." Silas had been nearby, but wasn't involved in our decisions on who to email.

"I'll take him out if Cole doesn't." Ivy put her napkin on her plate. "Are all wolves just born to be good cooks? Well, besides Silas and me?"

Cole snorted a laugh and put his arm around her. "I'm sure your food is edible. But I agree, that food was really good, Bone. If you ever get sick of this asshole, you're welcome in my pack." He nodded his chin in Silas's direction.

Bone was an excellent cook, although there were some grumbles about how long it took him to cook. Not as good as me, but I wasn't complaining.

"Once we get a good read on the pack, we can solidify our plans. The Tahoe pack is sending reinforcements to help in the next few days. So now we're just going to have to be patient." Sara stood and looked around. "Where will Manny and I be sleeping?"

"Manny and you?" My eyes lifted from the laptop and landed on Manny, who was staring up at Sara with a goofy look on his face. What the hell was going on? "Manny? What is she talking about?"

I was trying to keep my cool, but was having a hard time not lunging over the table and asking him what he was doing with her. Manny was a good guy, but not for my sister.

He looked at me and rubbed his jaw. "Well see, we can share a bed now because we're together."

I stood, the chair I was in falling backward. "No. You can't."

Sara rolled her eyes and stood with a wince. Her prosthetic must have been bothering her or she was having phantom pains again. "Yes, we can. We're grown adults. And besides, you're shacking up with a woman and three other men now, so you have no business worrying about my sex life."

"You two can take the room upstairs and we'll sleep in another room." Ivy grinned when Silas protested. "There's plenty of floor space in the room with the bunks to make one giant mattress."

"How long has this been going on?" When Manny shrugged in response, I leaned over the table and got in his face. "If you hurt her, I swear I'll-"

"You'll do nothing, Elias. Stop being overprotective. We're having fun." She smiled when Manny stood and wrapped his arm around her waist. "Goodnight, everyone. Thanks for dinner."

They headed up the stairs, and I turned to Cole. "Can you believe that?"

"They flirt all the time. I don't see why you're so surprised." Cole laughed. "I'm not ready for bed yet. One of those beanbags has my name written on it though."

I shut the laptop and looked over at the hallway leading to the other rooms. "I'm going to go check on Xander."

"What's his deal?" Silas started to help clear off the table from dinner dishes, but stopped and looked at Ivy for an answer.

"He showed up at Cole's house, stuck in his wolf form. He says he was taken with the rest of his pack." Ivy piled four plates on top of the four Silas already had. I hoped he didn't drop them.

"Taken by who?" A line formed between his brows. "And they took the whole pack? How is that possible?"

"I emailed a few packs in Washington to see if they know anything. Even if they aren't involved in our coalition, someone has to know about them." The table was just about cleaned off, so I left them and went to the bunkroom.

Knocking softly, I opened the door and peeked inside. Xander was on the bottom bunk. He was beautiful with the moonlight coming through the window and hitting the side of his face.

"Xander?" I shut the door quietly, not sure if I was going to frighten him.

"Hey." He scooted over and patted the spot next to him. "Come here."

"Did you eat the sandwich Ivy brought you?" I had no clue about Xander's thoughts on deer, so I was grateful Ivy had been looking out for him and made him a turkey sandwich.

"Yeah."

I took off my shoes and laid down on my side next to him, propping myself up on my elbow. "What happened earlier?"

Xander rolled onto his side to face me and slid an arm under the pillow. "I want that feeling. The feeling of seeing my pack mates again."

His eyes shut as I brought my hand to his cheek, a tear slipping down. I brushed it away with my thumb. "What can I do to help?"

"Kiss me." His eyes opened and glossy green eyes stared back at me. They reminded me of the forest.

"I... but we... I don't-" My blabbering didn't go on for long because he fisted my shirt, pulled me to him, and crashed his lips against mine.

Holy shit. A man was kissing me. A man who made me question what I was feeling and how my body was reacting to the softness of his lips and the hard lines of his body.

My hand fell from his cheek, landing on his wrist, clutching my shirt as if he was clinging on for dear life. And maybe he was.

I moved my lips against his, a deep groan tickling my lips as I gave in and let him have my mouth. His stubble rubbed against my skin and created a whole new sensation to kissing. A sensation my cock liked.

He rolled me onto my back, and I scooted over so I wouldn't fall off the bed. His body pressed into mine as his tongue invaded my mouth. I felt his excitement against my leg as his hand tangled in my hair, gently pulling my head to a better angle.

It had been a long time since I'd just made out with someone, and the fact that it was Xander made it ten times hotter. His lips made their way to just below my ear and then his mouth closed over my earlobe, biting it at the same time.

"God, Xander." My hands went to his ass, and I pulled him closer. "I never knew..."

His lips brushed the shell of my ear, and I shuddered. "Never knew what?" His teeth scraped down my neck to where my shoulder connected. "How good my lips would feel?"

I was about to bust a nut right in my pants with his raspy voice and roaming hands that were touching everywhere except my cock. The thought of him wrapping his hand around it again like he had in the treehouse made my erection jump in excitement.

He sucked the sensitive skin in the crease of my neck and then moved back to my lips, where he hovered so close it tickled. I stilled underneath him as our breath mingled and sparks felt like they were jumping between our lips.

"Why did you stop?" I ran my hand up and down his back.

"We're going too fast. You've never been with a man before. I don't want to pressure you." His lips brushed over mine, a long languid kiss taking the place of the frantic kiss we'd first shared.

This man... who was he?

"I'm a grown ass man, Xander."

"I know, but still." After a few lingering swipes of his mouth, he rolled to the side of me and pulled me against his chest. "I'm tired. Let's sleep."

I pulled away and sat up, ducking my head so I wouldn't hit it. "No."

"No?" One side of his mouth turned up in a sexy smile and his eyes trailed down tauntingly slow to my crotch. "What happened to your reservations earlier?"

I sucked in a breath and moved my hands to my pants, pulling out my erection. "This happened."

"Fuck, Eli." He rubbed his hand over his mouth. "Come here."

I laid on top of him, my hand between us, pumping my cock as he kissed me. I moved my lips to his neck and was overwhelmed by his scent. If I could nuzzle him and Ivy for the rest of my life, I'd be a lucky man.

"Take my cock out," he commanded, pulling my shirt off. "I want to feel you against me."

While I worked on freeing him from the confines of his pants, he pulled his shirt off. Despite what had happened to him, he still had muscle definition, and the light smattering of dark hair on his chest made him look even sexier.

I slid off my pants and then sat back on my heels, taking in the sight before me. I'd seen him naked already, but not like this. Not when both of us were hard for each other, cocks dripping and ready for release.

He seemed to be just as enamored with my body, his eyes a dark green in the moonlight from outside. I licked my lips and lowered my mouth to his thigh, kissing it.

"Eli, you don't have to- oh shit." His hips jackknifed off the bed as I kissed the tip of his cock.

I might not have given a blow job before, but I had my own first-hand experience to go off of. I kissed down his shaft and licked my way back up.

"Get it nice and slick. I want your cock sliding next to mine." His hands fisted my hair, and I took him in my mouth. "Ah, fuck, yes."

He hit the back of my throat and I sucked as I got him ready with my spit. I released him with a pop, and he yanked on my hair, pulling me up.

Our lips connected, and I groaned as he gripped both of us in his fist. The pressure was perfect; he was perfect. I didn't know what I had done to deserve both him and Ivy, but I wasn't about to complain.

"Xander, fuck. It feels amazing." I kissed down to his nipple and took it in my mouth. He gasped and his grip tightened. "Get us off. Let me feel you come all over me."

I wrapped my hand around his, our pre-cum slick as our hands glided over our cocks. Pressure built in the base of my spine and my balls, and before I could slow myself down, my orgasm rolled through me.

"Oh, shit. I'm coming." I groaned as I spilled all over our hands and stomachs.

"So. Sexy." His jaw clenched and his back arched as his own release took hold.

I rolled off him, my chest heaving. "That was..."

The door opened, light spilling in from the hall, and

Ivy walked in. Spotting us naked all sexed up in the bed, she shut the door quickly.

"Am I interrupting something?" She raised an eyebrow and went to the nightstand where a box of tissue was. "Jesus, there's cum everywhere."

She scrunched her nose, pulled a bunch of tissue out, and handed it to me. I felt like my cheeks were on fire as I wiped up the mess.

"I'm a little disappointed you didn't come in a few minutes ago." Xander chuckled and cleaned himself.

"You're okay with this?" I scooted to the edge of the bed so I could see her better. "I know you said you were, but..."

"Why wouldn't I be?" She sat down next to me. "There's enough love to go around, right?"

Love? I swallowed the lump of emotion in my throat.

Xander stifled a yawn. "We should get some sleep. Who knows what tomorrow will bring?"

And that was what scared me.

CHAPTER FOURTEEN

Ivy

Sleeping in was nearly impossible when you shared a room with three other people. Judging from the light shining through the window, it was at least seven in the morning, and all three men were already up.

Once things settled down, we were going to need to do some serious thinking about the sleeping arrangements. While I wasn't opposed to sharing one big bed, I was also realistic. Sometimes I needed my space, and they would want alone time with me too.

We would each need our own bedrooms and one to share. Cole's place had enough rooms for that to happen, but what about Silas? Would he want to move into Cole's house?

Pushing my grand plans aside, I slid out of bed, wondering what the day would bring. Cole and Silas would probably be busy figuring out what they were going to do about Dante. Dante not only brought a threat to Cole, but to the West Arbor Pack as well.

People like Dante wouldn't just give up taking over one pack, they'd want to take over them all. His commentary about wolves taking their rightful place was extremely concerning. Did that mean he wanted to out the wolves to all mankind?

If people knew wolves existed, they would start closely examining all phenomena. That would put the tritons and sirens at risk too. There were probably so many other creatures that existed that I didn't know about.

Since we would be working out, I put on some workout clothes Carly had let me borrow, and threw a t-shirt on over the top. The last thing I needed was for them to freak out over me in just a sports bra.

Who cared if they walked around without shirts half the time?

In the main living space of the den, Bone and Carly were lounging on the sectional with their phones.

"Girl, you look damn good in those capris." Carly and I had somewhat become friends. There were a few other females that hung around, but Carly seemed to be around the most.

Did it bother me she had slept with Silas? A little. She seemed like a cool chick, but a little lost in the man department. It wasn't like I could judge her when I'd been sleeping with three men, and probably would soon add a fourth.

"Eli's cooking us breakfast. He said he doesn't need any help. You're welcome to join us." Bone didn't look up from his phone. "Everyone else is checking the perimeter."

"I'll go check on Eli first." Maybe I could borrow a phone and call Riley and Jessica.

I left them and went into the kitchen where music was playing. Eli was standing at the stove, shaking his hips. Was he on the breakfast menu?

Trying to be sneaky, I tiptoed toward him, but damn wolf senses, he must have smelled me and turned to look over his shoulder. "Good morning, beautiful."

I had no clue what he was cooking, but it smelled delicious.

"Good morning." I grunted in protest when he turned and grabbed me around the waist and took my hand. "I don't dance."

He threw his head back and laughed. He was in a great mood, and it only improved my mood. This was the Eli I had first met, calm and relaxed.

"Well, I'll have to change that." He started moving, and I went along for the ride. I had no idea what he was leading me to do, but it involved a few sidesteps and some hip action. I was not a dancer at all, unlike my best friend, Riley, who did competitive ballroom dancing.

I would have thought the person who had no legs in their other form would suck at dancing, and the one with legs would be the better dancer. Wrong.

He sucked in a sharp breath when I stepped on his foot. Instead of moving, he just began swaying instead. "I've always liked a good challenge."

I smacked his chest playfully and he let me go, turning back to the stove and lifting the lid on a pot. Inside was boiling poblanos, tomatoes, onion, and other aromatics.

Eli was every woman's dream—he could cook, dance, and fuck—rolled into one sexy package.

"Maybe once we're back home, I'll let you teach me. I've taken a few lessons, but after every single one I wanted to curl up in a ball and cry." I leaned against the counter and watched as he cooked.

"It sounds like you just didn't have the right teacher." He turned off the stove and took the pot of boiling goodness to the sink where the blender container was.

Steam exploded upwards as he poured the boiled concoction into it. He moved the container to the blender base, put on the lid, and turned it on.

"What are you fixing?" I was so hungry I could have eaten a... fuck. I could have eaten a deer.

"Chilaquiles. Have you had it before?" He turned off the blender and removed the lid, the smell and steam wafting into the air.

"Can't say I have, but it smells delicious." My mouth watered as he dropped corn tortillas cut into fourths into a basket and dropped them in the fryer. "Chips? For breakfast?"

"It's really good. You cook them a little in the sauce

I just made and add fried egg with some beans on the side. You'll be craving it all the time." He shook the basket. "This is the way I make it."

"I can't wait to have more of your cooking. I make a mean mac and cheese… from the box." I was exaggerating a bit and could cook simple things, but it wasn't any fun to just cook for myself.

"I'll teach you how to make it from scratch. It's easy. You can follow directions, can't you?" He sounded like he was teasing me, probably because I hadn't followed their directions very well since meeting them.

"Of course, I can. If I choose to."

He took out the batch of chips and put in another. "I'll have to provide you with some incentive then."

"That might work." I grinned. "Do you get sick of taking care of the pack?"

He shrugged. "At first I did. Neither of my parents were the omega, and the previous one wasn't that great. So, when our wolves started showing their places in the pack, and Sara was clearly going to be the lowest, I decided it couldn't be that bad of a role. And it hasn't been besides having to fight my wolf about it."

"It's not that bad of a role unless you're dealing with wolves like Dante." I sighed. "Silas's pack doesn't have an omega. It seems that anybody that wants to be around him kind of takes care of the pack."

"It could also be whatever magic that has created us, trying to tell us we should all be one pack. I'm fairly certain that if the packs combined, Bone would not be a beta."

"How do you know?"

"My wolf knows. All of our wolves know their place in the pack. Most of the time we can get a sense of where a wolf ranks from another pack just from being around them. To my wolf, you're overwhelmingly alpha."

The only thing my wolf could sense was she was higher ranked than others. Maybe it was a learning process, and since my wolf had just come out to play, she would need time to learn all the intricacies of being a wolf.

"Do you think there are other types of shifters out there? Can you sense them?" I'd had no clue my best friend, who I'd grown up with, was different. But then again, neither did she.

Eli moved to the refrigerator and grabbed a carton of eggs. "When I went to college, I got a vibe from some people. There weren't very many, but when I looked at them or smelled them it was like my Spidey sense went off. I think the coalition probably knows if there are."

What the hell was the coalition?

I didn't want to pester him with too many questions about wolves, and I didn't want to overwhelm my brain with information, so I decided to bring up the night before. He had seemed sheepish after I came into the room, and I didn't want him to feel weird about it.

"So, last night actually happened, didn't it?" He handed me the empty container from the blender that he had just dumped into a pan, and I set it on the counter. "How... uh... was it?"

I was genuinely curious about his feelings toward Xander. Just like with me, things had moved rather quickly. It made me think other factors were at play other than just libido and attraction.

"You really want to talk about it? Doesn't it feel kind of like... I'm cheating?" He sounded very unsure of his words. Hell, I had the same feelings when I'd slept with him after already sleeping with Cole.

"No, we talked about it. If it was another female... geez, I sound like a hypocrite." I didn't even understand myself why I was okay with him being with another man, but if he were to suddenly have feelings for another female, I'd probably rip her head off.

"You don't. Maybe it's because all four of us are your mates. If I told you I wanted to do the same things with David, how would that make you feel?" Eli put chips into the sauce he had poured in the pan.

"First off, who the hell is David? And second, it makes me feel murderous."

He laughed. "David is Bone. Rover's name is Dax. Silas has an odd way of coming up with nicknames. David told me his is because the lead actor in the show *Bones* is David. And Rover? Because of Dax Shepard and the word Shepard reminded Silas of a dog."

"Say what?" It took me a minute to process that. "So how the hell did he arrive at bunny for me?"

"Maybe because your hair is red, and Jessica Rabbit has red hair? Nicknaming people like he does is endearing. David says it means he really cares about you." He chuckled and started cooking eggs. "If at any point you're uncomfortable with me exploring things with Xander, you need to tell me. It's just… I feel this connection with him, that goes beyond normal…"

That was exactly how I felt about my connection with all of them. It wasn't typical, but it was so strong I couldn't resist.

∽

Breakfast was delicious, but I expected nothing less from Eli. Since I "helped" him in the kitchen, I got out of doing dishes, and I wasn't going to argue otherwise.

"Come with me. I want to show you something." Eli took my hand and pulled me toward the door as everyone else cleaned up the table and went about their business.

"It's not how to dance, is it?" I was stuffed, and if he were about to teach me to dance, I would have probably puked. At breakfast, they had talked about working out in an hour or two, and I didn't even think my belly would be ready then.

We went out the back door and headed for the trees. Eli laced our fingers together and hummed softly as we entered the cover of trees. The last snowfall seemed to have brought on spring; the forest was coming alive with new growth.

Now that my senses were heightened, I could smell the animal life too. Luckily I didn't want to eat any of it since I was full. But who was I kidding? There was really only one thing my wolf wanted to eat.

"I haven't seen or heard about your wolves hunting any animals for food." I looked to the side, and he tried to hide a grin but wasn't successful. "What do you hunt and why do I get the feeling that my deer cravings aren't normal?"

"Our wolves can go a while without hunting. Yours seems to have a voracious appetite, but maybe that's because she's been locked away for so long. I enjoy a good squirrel. They satisfy my hunger and help my garden." He threw his head back and laughed when I scrunched my nose. "If you didn't fancy deer so much, I'd take you out squirrel hunting."

"Do they have a nutty flavor? Maybe squirrel can be dessert." It was a horrible joke, but how else does one who turns into a hunting machine deal with it? I was embracing it because otherwise I'd beat myself up over it.

"You aren't grossed out about all of this?" He rubbed his thumb over my hand. "It's okay if you are. When I was younger, I had a hard time the first time I hunted."

"At first I was, but I keep telling myself it's normal." I still had no clue where we were going, but we were getting farther and farther into the forest.

We eventually came to a small clearing that had a pool of water surrounded by rocks. "I saw this on Google maps a while back when I was scouting this territory. It's a hot spring. Care to join me?"

"You don't have to ask me twice." I kicked off my shoes and pulled my shirt over my head. "Is it safe?"

"Silas said it was." He pulled down his pants, revealing his toned ass that I really wanted to sink my teeth into. "I also asked him if his answer would change if I told him I was bringing you here."

"And did it?" I pulled off my sports bra and Eli's eyes lit up. "Don't get that look in your eye, I'm so stuffed from breakfast there will be no hanky-panky going on in the hot spring."

"Of course not. That really might be dangerous." He walked to the edge of the water and dipped his toe in. "It's warm here at the edge. Silas said the temperature was bearable but not to stay in too long."

I shucked the rest of my clothes and took his outstretched hand. We waded into the warm water until we were about mid-chest. My entire body warmed up and my muscles relaxed.

"This is really nice. Thanks for bringing me here." I dipped down in the water a little so it would come to my neck.

Eli was quiet and glided his hands across the surface. Something was on his mind, and it wasn't of the light-hearted variety. We'd been having such a good time all morning, and now he was suddenly serious.

"I'm worried about Cole. He's different… subdued, quiet." Eli shook his head and wrapped his arms around me, pulling me close. "I know it might be hard for you to tell because you haven't known him for very long, but he almost seems depressed."

"He's been through a lot. Have you asked him about it?" I put my head against his chest as he rubbed my back in small circles.

"I mentioned it, and he snapped at me. He told me nothing was wrong, and I should try being shot in the stomach." He put his cheek on the top of my head. "Maybe he just needs time."

"I'm sure it's been a lot for him to deal with. I can try talking to him." I was already feeling overheated from the hot water and the proximity of Eli. "This is really great, but I kind of feel like my blood is boiling right now, and I need to get out."

"Oh, thank God. I was feeling the same way from the second we got in." We waded out and looked at our dry clothes that sat on a rock.

"What should we do while we wait for our bodies to dry?" I looked around and wiggled my eyebrows. "Want to fool around?"

"What if someone sees?" He pulled me close, my breasts pushing against his chest. "And where?"

"No one's going to see. But if they do, who cares." I moved my hand between us and grabbed his dick. "What do you mean where? You fucked me in the shower. I think we can figure out how without lying down."

I guided him backward as I worked my hand up and down his shaft, bringing him to life. His breaths were already heavy, and his eyes hooded. "How could I forget?"

His back hit a tree and then his lips were on mine with bruising intensity. I gasped in surprise as his arms wrapped around me, his fingers digging into the globes of my ass.

My core was already throbbing with need, and I worked my hand harder as his cock grew in size. He kissed down to my neck, sucking and nipping at my sensitive skin.

"You taste so good... I should've had you for breakfast." His fingers dug into my flesh and he lifted me, my legs wrapping around him. "This time I want you facing me."

"Is that so?" My hands looped around the back of his neck. "Are we going to fuck just like this?"

Once I was holding on to him tightly, he lifted me up further with one arm and reached between us, lining his cock up with my entrance and lowering me onto him.

"Hold on tight." He bounced me on his dick, and I cried out. "Does that feel good?"

"So good." I used him as leverage as he slid me up and down his shaft. I'd never had sex in such a position before, and it was a whole different sensation to have my feet off the ground.

His powerful arms and legs supported me as we both drew closer to our peaks. It was as if our bodies were meant for what we were doing.

Sensing he was close and wanting to come with him, I reached between us and rubbed my clit. The faster he moved me, the faster I rubbed, until we were both crying out with nothing surrounding us but the trees.

I clung to him, burying my face in his shoulder as he lowered my trembling legs to the ground. I was probably the most satisfied woman in the world with four men to lavish me with attention. How did I get so lucky?

Eli pulled away and led me to our clothes. "What's that goofy grin for?"

"Just thinking about how an unlucky situation turned out to be just what I needed." And it was true.

When my parents died, I lost a part of myself. I lost a family that loved and cherished me. But in that drawer in my dad's desk had been a gift.

The map to a new family.

CHAPTER FIFTEEN

Ivy

Waiting around was doing nothing to help keep the anxiety that was forming a tight ball in my stomach away. We should have been doing something, anything really, to remove Dante from his place of power. He could do a lot of damage to the pack and the entire wolf kind in a short time if we didn't act fast.

There couldn't be that many wolves on his side, could there?

I stared at Riley's number pulled up on Sara's phone and considered what I was going to tell her. If I said the wrong thing, she'd show up in Arbor Falls, and that was the last thing we needed.

"Hello?" Her voice sounded tired when she answered, and I straightened in my seat on the couch.

"Ri? What's wrong?" It was eleven o'clock in the morning and Riley wasn't one to sleep in. She helped run a nonprofit ocean cleanup organization and was always up and raring to go before the sun rose.

"Ivy! Where the hell have you been? You better tell me that a hot man or men have had you in their fuck nest and holding you hostage with their fancy peens or I'm going to be mad, and you know how stabby I get when I'm mad." She had perked up some, but didn't sound like her normal self.

"Fuck nest? Where did that come from?" I laughed and cringed when Manny looked over from where he and Sara were doing something on the laptop at the table. "And there are four peens now, by the way."

"Four? Girl. I can hardly handle three. A fuck nest is where demons mate... it was in a book I just finished. I told the guys we needed a fuck nest like the main character, but now I don't know." She cleared her throat. "Where have you been, and do I need to come save you?"

"I'm fine. Now you don't know if you need one? What's going on with you? Do I need to come save *you*?"

"Something's brewing, but I'm not sure what exactly. The guys have been called to the city on guard rotations." She sighed. I couldn't blame her for being upset. She didn't like living under the water where the city was located. "They're only called when something is going on and more of them are needed."

"And what about you? They didn't call you?" She

was a siren, so if something was going on, she would have been called too.

"Well." Another sigh. "I can't because I'm pregnant."

"What?" I jumped out of my seat, my voice echoing through the building. "When? How? When are you due?"

She laughed. "I think we know how, Ivy. We've been trying, I just didn't want to say anything until it happened and everything was okay. I'm twelve weeks."

"This is so exciting! Congratulations! Oh my God, that means I'm going to be an aunt!" I was squealing and was not ashamed. "Wait. How is the water situation going to work?"

Riley and her mom didn't have to stay in the water, although it made them calmer and their lives longer. On the other hand, tritons were born in water and had to train to shift and be on land.

"Right now we're waiting to see if I need to move underwater… a siren and triton have never had babies together before to anyone's knowledge." She sounded scared and my heart went out to her. "The main thing is that he or she is healthy and happy. If that means I have to move, so be it."

"I'm sure it will all work out. You know that Jax, Morgan, and Blake will take care of you and protect you one hundred percent." I hoped my men were as devoted to me as Riley's men were to her.

We talked for a little longer about Cole, Eli, Xander, and Silas without me giving too much information away, and I reassured her everything was fine. Now I really needed to make sure she didn't end up coming to

Arbor Falls since she was pregnant. The last thing we needed was the wrath of the tritons and sirens coming down on us if something happened to her.

She could definitely hold her own, but getting in the middle of a wolf battle wouldn't be good considering her strength was in the water.

After talking to Jessica and making sure she also knew I was fine and just going through a quarter life crisis, I wandered outside to see what everyone was doing.

The guys had headed out to train before I got on the phone, and as much as I had wanted to join them, I also had to make sure my human business was taken care of. The bills didn't stop just because I wasn't at home or because I wasn't a human.

On the far side of the property was a metal barn, but I couldn't smell horses or other farm animals. The large metal doors were open, and music came from inside.

I looked down at myself, wondering if I should go change. Carly had given me a pair of yoga pants and a sports bra, but last time I wore something revealing to work out, I nearly started a riot.

Screw that. If they couldn't handle my comfort, they could go suck Dante's big toe.

I stopped at the entrance and my eyes widened. It had what you'd expect in a gym, but it also had an octagon, several punching bags, and dummies. It made me want to crack my knuckles.

"Bunny." Silas jogged over to me wearing a pair of black workout shorts and nothing else. His chest and forehead were beaded with sweat, and his hair was pulled back in the tiniest ponytail ever. "I was just telling Cole that I thought you could kick his ass."

He threw his sweaty arm around my shoulders and led me over to where Cole was punching a heavy punching bag hanging from a metal beam. With every punch, he exhaled a short, quick breath. He was dressed in the same thing as Silas.

I was not complaining about the view.

"I'm not fighting her. I bet she fights dirty and goes straight for the nuts." Cole did some combo that made my head spin and then stopped and shook out his hands. "But I wouldn't mind grappling around a bit." He wiggled his eyebrows and did a sweep of me with his eyes.

I shoved away from Silas, who laughed as I walked away. Thankfully, the two of them weren't bickering.

Xander and Eli stood just outside another door, and I went to join them. My jaw dropped to the floor as I watched Carly shoot an arrow at a target at the other end of a small field. She didn't hit the bullseye, which was right over the heart of a dummy, but she got close.

"What are we doing, boys?" I moved out in front of them and Eli wrapped his arms around me, putting a hand flat against my stomach.

I'd never seen a bow up close before, and it was much larger than I thought. Carly looked badass shooting it, and my fingers itched to try.

"We're supposed to be lifting weights, but we got distracted by Katniss over there." Xander nodded his chin at Carly. "She's pretty good."

"Have you guys tried it before?" I already knew I was going to try it if she'd let me. How could I not?

"Nope."

"Never."

"You guys are throwing off my focus with all your chatter." Carly held the bow at her side and looked over her shoulder. "Want to try?"

"I thought you'd never ask." I skipped over to her like a kid going to Disneyland. "I've never done it before."

She raised the bow up. "It's simple, really. This is a recurve bow, and the first thing you do is attach your thumb to the finger sling. Then get an arrow." She pulled an arrow out of her quiver. "You put three fingers on the string. One finger above the arrow and two below."

I wasn't sure what she told me next because a weird feeling, kind of like déjà vu, came over me, and the next thing I knew, she was handing me the bow. What the hell was that all about? I completely blanked out for a solid minute.

I took it, and without thinking, grabbed an arrow, raised the bow, and shot at the target, the arrow hitting right in the middle of the bullseye.

"What the hell? I thought you said you'd never shot before?" Carly huffed. "Probably was beginner's luck."

A weird calmness washed over me, and I held out my hand for another arrow. She handed me one, and I did the same thing, the arrow landing right in the bullseye. It was so close to the other arrow that they could have been conjoined twins. I didn't even know how I was doing it.

"Do you have any moving targets?" Xander had come to stand next to me at some point and was staring at me in awe.

"Yeah. Give me a few minutes." Carly jogged off to a small shed and went inside.

"Why are you staring at me like that?" I glanced at Xander out of the corner of my eye as I examined the bow more closely.

"Just thinking."

That wasn't vague at all. I was about to question him further when Carly came back out with a remote-controlled car and a ceramic rabbit. Cole and Silas wandered out of the barn to join us.

"What's going on out here?" Cole wiped the sweat off his forehead with his forearm. "We heard someone say you have the perfect shot."

Great. An even bigger audience.

It wasn't that I was shy, but it *was* kind of weird I could just do something perfectly. Carly wasn't a perfect shot, and she clearly had done it a lot, so why could I do it on the first try?

"Bullseye twice! I've never seen someone do that without warming up. Especially not when they've never done it before." Carly was busy strapping the ceramic rabbit to the top of the car.

"Let's see this for ourselves." Silas rubbed his hands together. "Time for my bunny to shoot some bunnies."

"Is that why you call me bunny? Because you want to use me for target practice?" I narrowed my eyes at him. "You wanted to kill me the first time you saw me?"

"What? No, bunny. Never." He took my cheeks in his hands. "I would never hurt you."

"Then why?" I knew I had him right where I wanted him. I didn't mind the nickname, but if it was some ridiculous jab at me, I didn't want it.

His eyes searched mine, and he bit his lip. "You won't let me call you it anymore."

"Well, that's for sure since you won't tell me why."

He flinched. "It's because of your hair, okay? You know how people call redheads carrot tops and bunnies like carrots?" He let me go and backed up a step. Smart man. "And it just kind of tumbled from my lips. It's cute, right?"

"My hair isn't even that shade of red." I was going to shoot an arrow at him. I'd determined a long time ago that people were jealous of redheads and blondes, that's why we were always the brunt of hair color jokes.

When had anyone ever made a joke about a brunette? Never.

"In the right light-" Cole shut his mouth when I glared at him.

"You can pick my nickname. How about that? I've never let anyone besides Coco give me one, and that's only because he's too lazy to say Silas."

"Okay. From now on I'm going to call you lass... or maybe ass." I smirked, and everyone laughed except Silas. "Yeah, I think lass is fitting since you have long hair."

"Now, wait just a second. A nickname doesn't have

to be from my actual name. You know what? I changed my mind." He crossed his arms over his chest, and I almost forgot what we were talking about with the way his muscles flexed. "Silas. Say it with me. Si-las with an uh sound, not an ah sound."

"Nope. Too late. Now, lass, go ahead and back up so I can shoot at this poor bunny someone painstakingly made only to have it slaughtered by my arrow."

Carly shook her head and laughed, putting the bunny target down and using the remote control to drive it out into the shooting field. "Okay, girl. Show this bunny who's boss."

Grabbing another arrow, I watched the target, raised the bow, and let it fly. The target flipped onto its side, the wheels spinning in the air. I didn't know how it was possible, but it was.

I turned to my onlookers and shrugged my shoulders as they stared at me open-mouthed. "I guess I just found a new talent."

"That's impossible." Silas jogged out to the downed target, picking it up and examining it. "Right in the heart!"

"It's not beginner's luck, that's for sure." Carly adjusted her ponytail. "Makes me wonder how you'll do shooting a gun. I'm going to go get one!"

Before I could protest, she ran off to get a gun. I wasn't a fan of them, but I was curious if I could hit the bullseye or if it was just limited to arrows.

"Are you just fucking with us?" Silas pulled the arrow out of the busted rabbit. "I mean, I would expect you to have a shorter learning curve because of your wolf capabilities, but never having shot before and hitting target after target?"

"I swear I have never picked up a bow before." I handed the bow back to Carly as she returned with a gun. I had the strangest urge to hug it to my chest and not let it out of my sight.

She showed me how to shoot the gun and I cringed. The sound itself was enough to make me piss myself, but I needed to see if I could shoot a gun accurately too.

Taking it, I did exactly as she directed, pointing it at the same dummy target in the middle of the field. I pulled the trigger and had no clue where the bullet went.

"That was horrible." Carly took the gun back from me. "I guess your weapon is a bow and arrow."

"Maybe we can order me one and I can practice. Although, I don't know what purpose it would have if I can just hunt as a wolf. Maybe I can go for the Olympics? Enter some competitions?"

"Well, that's great and all, but one of the coalition's laws is no wolf can engage in any competitive sport in which financial gain is received or attention is drawn to our abilities." Eli rocked back on his heels. "They will behead you if you take part."

My eyes widened and everyone nodded. "Wh... what?"

"You should see your face right now. Priceless." Cole put his arm around me. "No one is beheading anyone. Packs can be fined if their members use their abilities in any way that might draw attention to our kind."

"I played volleyball and received some titles and awards. Does that mean there's going to be a surprise collection notice that shows up one day with a hefty fine?" I had been a star volleyball player, and come to think of it, I hadn't put in as much work as some of my teammates. I just assumed I was a natural and left it at that.

"Probably not..." He stopped, a frown on his face. "I don't know what they're going to say or do when we report your existence."

"Wait a hot damn second. You haven't contacted the coalition yet?" Silas put his hands on his hips. "I thought you were Mr. Goody Two Shoes and followed the laws."

Cole rolled his eyes, which I noticed he did a lot around Silas. It was odd seeing a grown man roll his eyes in such an annoyed way at another man. "Between chasing her down the few times she tried to run, getting her situated and making sure she wasn't going to go feral, and Dante, I haven't exactly had the time."

"I'm sure it will be fine." Xander sighed. "They are all talk."

Silas turned to Eli. "The last thing we need is them catching wind of everything on their own. To them, all they'll see is a wolf that is different from the rest of us magically appearing out of nowhere and a coup against one of the stronger alphas in the Western states."

"What did I tell you about telling my omega what to do?" Cole was back to being grumpy. Maybe that would be my nickname for him.

"I wasn't telling him. I was suggesting he do the

right thing. Besides. He's a free-floating omega now, isn't he? He has no pack and neither do you."

Cole stepped right into Silas's chest, his head tilted in a confrontational angle. "Fuck. You."

I wasn't sure who shoved who first, but before any of us could intervene, they were throwing punches. Xander attempted to pull Cole away but got elbowed in the jaw. Some of the others in the gym came outside and began egging them on.

A shrill whistle pierced our ears and made me want to cover them. "Enough!" Silas's grandfather, Pops, as he called him, stood at the open door, looking as mean as ever.

Silas gave Cole one last shove, and Cole elbowed Silas in the ribs as they stood next to each other. They reminded me of two bickering brothers. Maybe one day they would get over themselves and get along, otherwise, we were going to have words.

"Just the man I wanted to see." Workout forgotten, I headed toward him, his eyes narrowing on me in the same way they had at breakfast the day before. "We need to talk."

Grumbling to himself, he turned and headed off down the side of the barn and across the yard, staying well away from the helicopter parked in the center. I followed like a dog after a bone, the guys close behind me.

Not even turning around, he raised his hand in a *stop right there* gesture. "The woman only."

"If you think I'm going to let her go into the forest

alone with you-" Cole started and then grunted as Silas put his arm out and clotheslined him to a stop.

"Pops might be scary as fuck, but he won't hurt her." Silas sped up and walked backward in front of me. "Do you want one of us to come with you? I don't want you to feel uncomfortable."

I waved him off. Pops was just a disgruntled old man, nothing I couldn't handle. "I'll scream if I need help."

Whatever he was going to tell me had to be serious if he was leading me into the woods away from everyone... or was that just a way to get me alone so he could murder me?

"Girl, I'm not going to hurt you." He looked over his shoulder. "You don't want anyone to hear your business, do you?"

I caught up with him. "No, but where are we going?"

"To where my son found you."

CHAPTER SIXTEEN

Ivy

We walked much longer than I thought we would. I heard running water and my heart jumped into my throat. I slowed and looked at Pops, who had been silent since telling me where we were headed.

"What is it, pup?" He slowed to match my step. "Does this place feel familiar to you?"

"Just reminds me of almost dying a few days ago." I sighed. "We're headed to the river?"

"Near it, yes." He tilted his head back a little and sniffed before changing his trajectory to the right. "We're almost there."

It was peaceful walking through the forest with him. I'd been quick to judge him as a grumpy old man, but maybe he was just lonely and needed company.

"Why would someone abandon me in the woods? Do you think it's because I'm different?" When he didn't answer me, I stopped and grabbed his arm. "Why do you think I'm different? Am I something other than a wolf?"

He looked down at my hand on his flannel shirt and then up at me with narrowed eyes. "I think you need to get your hand off me, child."

I dropped my hand like he was a lump of hot coal and stepped away from him. "Should I call for my mates?"

"It's only a little farther." He started walking again, not sparing me another glare. "I don't like being touched."

I kept my distance, more cautious of him now. He stopped in front of a group of boulders, not far from the river.

"Is this where I was found?" Seemed like a horrible place to abandon a newborn, but maybe my mother didn't have any other choice.

"Yes." He pointed to an area between the boulders that would have provided adequate coverage to a baby. "He said he heard you crying a mile away. He was on patrol that night."

I crossed my arms over my chest. "I think my father was Baron."

He shielded his eyes from the sun and squinted at me. His jaw worked back and forth as he examined my face. "He wouldn't have abandoned you if he was your father. Baron was a good man."

"He was found dead the day after I was born. I was

placed in an ivy bush outside a clinic and found that same morning. I'm guessing your son put me there?" He was considering the information I shared. "Why not take me to the women of the pack? Or the alpha?"

"You didn't smell like a wolf. I asked him the same questions when he told me years and years ago. I didn't know the connection between your birth and Baron's death." He dropped his hand and stared out at the river. "My son was secretive."

Was. Did he not think he was alive anymore?

"He paid a social worker five hundred thousand dollars about a week later to ensure I was adopted far away from here." Something was amiss, and I intended to dig all I needed to in order to find the answers.

That surprised him, and he brought his hand to his chest. "Excuse me."

"Half a million-"

"We didn't have that kind of money." He shook his head vehemently. "Where would he have gotten that kind of cash?"

"Maybe he robbed a bank, or like you said, he was secretive." Unlike the movies, there weren't a ton of ways a person could get that kind of cash quickly. Did he just have that much lying around somewhere?

Movement drew my attention to the trees where Silas was walking toward us. "He had it hidden in the floorboards of the house, Pops."

That was a surprise to me. He hadn't said a word about it and had acted like they had none. Had he been lying?

"I thought I told you-" The grumpy face was back. I

wondered what his story was. Maybe part of it was because his son left.

"She's my mate. You don't really expect me to leave her alone with another man for long, do you?" He wrapped his arm around my waist and pulled me into his side. "Why did you bring her out here?"

"This is where she was abandoned. Tell me everything you know about that money." His eyes darkened, and he looked out at the river again.

"He was kind of frantic getting it out. There were two metal boxes, and inside were bundled bills. I was like eight, so I don't remember much else. He was very short with me, and I went back to my room."

"It could have been your mother's money. She was always saying nonsense about needing to be prepared for anything and everything." He seemed tired suddenly and looked back to the forest like he wanted to go back.

"But half a million dollars? That's life savings level." Silas scratched his beard. "I wish we had a way to contact him."

"He just... left?" I was already growing more and more concerned about what had actually happened to my real mother and father. Something bad had gone down.

"Yeah. He said he was tired of pack life and wanted to travel." Silas shrugged. "I can't blame him. Between starting a new pack and dealing with Cole's father... I've only been doing this about ten years and I've about had it."

It sounded an awful lot like Silas hadn't heard from him since he had left. "Is he missing?"

"Yes." Pops looked at Silas with sadness in his eyes. "Now I'm thinking there's something else going on we don't know about."

"No." Silas crossed his arms over his chest. "He said he needed to find himself again. Being an alpha sucked the life out of him."

"Almost a decade with no contact is not needing to find himself again. He's missing or dead." Pops was not shitting around and pointed his finger at Silas. "You need to realize that and put him in that database doohickey. I'd do it myself if I had access and knew how."

"It can't hurt. Ten years is a long time, Silas." When I looked up at him, he wouldn't meet my stare. Maybe he was in denial.

One thing was for sure, he had the answers I needed.

∽

"I'm bored." I flopped down on the couch and propped my feet up. "Can't we get out of here for a while until the reinforcements arrive?"

After the revelations from the day before, we'd spent the rest of the day trying to find anything in Silas's house that might give us answers. We found nothing. I'd tossed and turned most of the night, trying to wrap my brain around how someone could abandon a baby in a forest.

Had I been abandoned there before or after Baron was murdered?

"We can watch Manny give Silas a tattoo." Cole chuckled and rubbed his hands together. "I'm sure that will be entertaining."

"What?" Silas paled as he came to join us. We had just eaten breakfast, cleaned the dishes, and checked emails. The replies so far were promising, but they could have also been lying.

Since when had my life become an episode of some crime drama?

"Time to get some ink. The needle doesn't hurt too much, and you heal quickly. Hardly any blood. Come on, you know you want one. Maybe a little bunny rabbit on your ass cheek." Cole was a completely different person around Silas. It was hard to describe, but he acted like a kid, not a leader of a pack in his mid-thirties.

But what did I know? I could be immature myself. Where was the fun in life if you were serious all the time?

Silas sat down heavily next to me. "You bastard. Stop talking about needles."

"What's wrong?" I turned to him, putting my hand on his leg. "You look like you're going to be sick."

Cole sat down on the other side of me, stretched, and put his arm around my shoulders. "Silas is scared of needles."

"Well, I think he's sexy enough without tattoos. If he got any, I'd have to beat off all the wolfettes that would come knocking on his door." I put my head against

Cole's arm. "Stop being mean to the poor boy or I'll have to cheer him up."

"You think I'm sexy?" Silas smirked and slid his hand around my waist, pulling me toward him. "Am I sexier than Cole?"

"This isn't a competition." Cole smoothed a hand over his hair, which only made me laugh. "But if it was, I'm certain I'm sexier than you, even on my bad days."

Silas used his free hand to smooth his beard. "It isn't a competition because there is no competition, Coco. Women can't resist the beard."

They were both so full of themselves, trying to one up each other. That could make for some interesting activities in the bedroom, though. "If you both don't stop, you'll both lose."

"Lose what? Their dicks?" Xander joined us, sitting on another sectional.

"Thinking about it, but I don't want to clean up the mess." I stood. "Let's do something. We can't just sit around here all day. What do you do every day, anyway?" Silas, of course, was the alpha, but he didn't have anywhere near the numbers Cole did.

"I need to run an errand in Huntsville. You can come with me." Silas sounded almost shy, which was such an odd thing for him. The man didn't seem to have a shy bone in his body.

Cole's chest rumbled. "I don't think that's a good idea."

"There are eyes on Dante. It's not like he's going to make it all the way to Huntsville without someone knowing. And if he does, what's he going to do in public?" Silas had a point, but Dante was also crazy, so who knew what he'd do in broad daylight.

"You can always come along if you have an issue with it. Maybe we can pick up some clothes while we're there, but you'll have to pay." I didn't even want to bother asking to go to my house. I didn't have much left there anyway besides clothes that didn't fit anymore or were the wrong season.

"I told Sara and Eli that we'd go over some video footage and strategize where we're going to infiltrate from." Cole stood and gave me a quick kiss before he looked down at Silas. "Don't be stupid."

"I'll go too. To keep an eye on Silas." Xander fist bumped Cole as he left to go find Sara and Eli. "But I could use some clothes of my own."

It was nice to see them getting along when at first I thought they were going to rip each other's throats out. Now, if Silas and Cole could just do the same, we'd be one happy bunch.

~

"So, tell us again, what's in these boxes?" I took one from the trunk of Silas's SUV and stood out of the way so he and Xander could grab the other two. They were the size of small moving boxes and were probably around twenty pounds.

Silas had been vague about what we were delivering, saying it was extra income for the pack. I didn't want to think it was something illegal, but he *had* been mad about the room he kept them in being left unlocked.

"You'll think differently of me. It's better if you don't know." He shut the trunk door, and we followed him as he rounded the corner of the building we were parked behind.

We were downtown, where mom and pop shops lined the streets and tourists enjoyed a day strolling around, buying things they probably didn't need. Huntsville was a tourist trap thanks to it being at the edge of a ski resort.

It wasn't too busy yet, since it was still morning and a weekday, but by noon it would be bustling. Some schools were probably on spring break, and with the snowstorm a few days prior, the slopes would be packed.

"Can we get arrested for what's in these?" Xander scanned the street and sidewalks as we walked. He'd been quiet the thirty-minute drive into town, his eyes glued to the scenery as we zoomed down the highway.

"No. I know it might seem that way, but it's just... personal." Silas stopped in front of a smoke shop and opened the door. "This should be quick."

"Please tell me there's not marijuana in these boxes." Weed was legal in California, but I was sure there was a right way to grow and sell it, and a wrong way.

"I think we'd smell it." Xander laughed and waited for me to enter in front of him.

The shop was pretty large, and from a quick glance around, it sold all types of smoking paraphernalia. It had everything from hookahs, to pipes, to what looked like every flavor of tobacco known to man. In the back of the shop was a fancy door that had *Cigar Room* in gold letters.

Silas headed for the back counter where a man was scrolling through his phone and set his box down. "Derek, how are you?"

"Silas! Glad to see you, man." They shook hands as Xander and I put our boxes down on the counter. "We've been running low on some of our best sellers. You have perfect timing."

Derek pulled a box cutter out and sliced open a box. Silas shifted from one foot to another. "We're kind of pressed for time. Everything's there."

Xander and I quickly glanced at each other and turned our attention back to the box, which was now open. Derek pulled out a small box that was inside and slid it open, a whistle leaving his mouth.

"Beautiful." He put it down on the counter without shutting it and we inched closer. "These bad boys are going to fly off the shelves."

The bad boy he was referring to was a ceramic pipe in the shape of a penis. The head was where a smoker would put their mouth and the bowl at the other end was shaped like balls. There were even veins on the thing. I bit my lip in an attempt not to laugh.

Xander grinned and picked up the box. "Are these handmade or do you buy them from China?"

Silas made a noise in his throat. "Handmade. I make things other than penises; these sell really well though."

"The man is a genius. They come in every color." Derek pulled out a check ledger and wrote Silas a check. "He sells on Etsy too. His shop is called *Wangs and Thangs.*"

"What are the thangs you sell?" I was quite surprised by these revelations about Silas. But I was also glad that the boxes didn't contain something illegal.

"Animals, food objects, some regular sculpted pieces." He shrugged. "It's no big deal. Let's go." Silas put the check in his wallet and led us out of the shop.

His face was slightly pink, and I took his hand, holding onto it as we walked out of the shop and down the sidewalk. It was a nice morning, the sun shining brightly and the smell of spring in the air. It was nice to forget about everything going on for a while and unwind. I just wished Eli and Cole had joined us.

Xander took my other hand as we walked. "I think it's cool you make ceramic penises people suck on. Do you put on *Unchained Melody* while you sit at your pottery wheel?"

Silas groaned and opened the door to a shop that sold women's clothing. "People pay fifty dollars apiece for penis pipes. How can I miss that opportunity when it takes me twenty minutes tops to mold and paint them?"

"Do you make pots and stuff like that?" I'd never been crafty because I didn't have the patience to spend hours and hours learning or to complete something that took painstaking detail.

"Vases and stuff." He let go of my hand to go to a rack of blouses. "You would look hot in this."

He held up an emerald green top that had a deep plunging neckline. I raised a brow and took it from him. "I was thinking of just getting simple stuff since I'm liable to ruin all my clothes."

"You'll get better at it as time goes on. When there isn't danger everywhere, you won't ruin so much." He picked up a sweater that had some weird cutouts down the arms. "This is already ripped for you."

I laughed and took my size off the rack. "Let's find some simple shirts and pants. Nothing crazy."

After trying on the clothes and buying the ones that worked, we headed to the next shop over for Xander. He went straight for the flannel section and chose just about every option they had.

"Now that we have the lumberjack all taken care of, let's get something to eat. I'm starving." Silas looked both ways and crossed the two-lane street that ran through the heart of Huntsville.

"I could go for some-" Xander stopped as soon as we were on the sidewalk.

"Xander?" I turned just as the bags he was carrying fell to the ground. "What's wrong?"

His eyes were closed, and his jaw locked so tightly that I worried he was going to get lockjaw. His hands were balled in fists, and before I could even process the blood dripping from them onto the sidewalk, Silas was shoving him down between two parked cars.

"Fuck! Stand on the other side in case someone walks by." Silas was standing next to the passing cars, trying to block the view of Xander shifting.

"They're here."

CHAPTER SEVENTEEN

Ivy

"What do you mean they're here?" I was too worried to talk to Xander in my head. It still took a certain amount of focus, which at that moment, I didn't have.

He didn't respond, and I looked helplessly at Silas, who was trying to keep him from escaping from between the two cars. What were we going to do? It was only a matter of time before someone noticed a wolf in the middle of town and went apeshit over it.

A few weeks ago, if I'd seen a wolf in the middle of town, I would have too.

"Damn it. I have tranquilizers in the SUV. I should have listened to my gut and put one in my pocket. We're going to have to knock him out then pretend he's a dog." Silas lunged for Xander, but Xander was fast and slipped past him, taking off down the sidewalk.

Dropping my bags between the cars, I ran after Silas who was sprinting faster than I knew was possible. If the giant wolf running through town didn't attract attention, the man sprinting after him at inhuman speed would.

"Xander! Stop right now! Bad dog! Sit!" Silas was practically to him when he darted across the street, causing a driver to slam on their brakes and honk their horn. Thank God the speed limit through town was twenty-five, and she had time to stop.

Silas held up his hand in apology and continued after the wayward wolf. With Silas screaming at him and calling him a dog, people just moved out of the way.

Everyone was watching the scene unfold in the streets of Huntsville. It would no doubt end up on social media if it went on for much longer. I could already see people going for their phones.

By some miracle, or maybe not so much of one, a shop door opened and Xander darted inside, nearly knocking a woman down as she exited. At least we had him corralled now and might be able to get him to shift back.

The bell chimed as I ran in after Silas, making sure the door shut behind me. There weren't too many people in the shop, and the manager was behind the counter, glaring at Silas, who was trying to head off Xander. He was like a bull in a china shop, except he was in a ski shop.

"This is why there are leash laws, you know. Do I need to call animal control?"

"No!" We both shouted at the same time.

Xander darted under a circular clothing rack with ski pants hanging on it. "Come on, buddy. Let's go to the car and this can all be over. I know you're scared. Do you want a treat?"

Silas was doing a great job at getting people to think we were dealing with our naughty dog because I heard no whispers about a wolf.

I would have squatted down to help, but people were pulling out their phones. "Please, put the phones away. My husband works for a special branch of the military and if you post any video or pictures of him, the FBI will shut your accounts down. I don't want for that to happen."

It seemed I was always having to think on my feet when I was with Silas and come up with a scenario to get us out of a situation. No one wanted their social media accounts taken away, so the phones didn't come out, at least from what I could tell.

"Can you talk to him in that special way only you can do, bunny?" Silas stood and gestured toward the rack.

I took his place and peeked in between the pants. It nearly broke my heart seeing him cowering against the metal support in the middle, his tail tucked and ears back.

"Sweetie, we need to get you out of here. Do you think you can handle that?" I wanted to reach out and touch him so badly, but the look in his eyes gave me pause.

He didn't respond. My stomach flipped over, and tears welled in my eyes. What the hell was going on and did we need to be concerned someone had found him somehow? That seemed impossible, though.

"Nothing. He's not responding." I gave Silas a helpless look. "How far is the car?"

"I can go get it. It's in the lot behind this building. I'm sure they won't mind if we use the back door if that'll get him out of here." He cleared his throat and then his voice was in my head. *"If he shifts, make sure no one sees him."*

Silas ran his plan by the manager, and he left the counter to let Silas out the back. Xander made no move besides the tremble of his body and quick jerks of his head when there was a sound in the shop.

"This was such a bad idea." I never had given any thought to Xander having an anxiety attack in public or what would happen if one of us shifted. It could have been me hovering under the rack.

"Ma'am?" A male voice boomed from behind me, and I stood just as Silas walked back in. "You dropped these bags out on the sidewalk."

"Thanks." I grabbed them and turned back to Silas. "How are we going to do this?"

"I'll carry him." He pushed more pants to the side. "Unless you have a better idea."

"That sounds like the best option." I looped the bags over my wrist.

"That man is lingering in the store. I don't like the smell of him." Silas squatted down. *"Let me try to get him out, and if he shifts, I might need you to create a diversion."*

I casually looked around, and sure enough, the man, who I hadn't even gotten a good look at honestly, was lingering by a wall of snowboards. *"Let's be quick."* We were lucky we could communicate silently.

"All right, bud. Let's get you out of here, okay? I'm going to carry you and make sure you're safe. I'll put you in the front seat too and then you can stick your head out the window on the way back home." Silas spoke in such a calm and hushed voice that it made my heart swell.

Silas moved into the rack and then emerged from the other side, Xander in his arms. He was speaking to him in a hushed tone that I couldn't hear as I followed him to the back of the store.

The back of my neck prickled, and I turned and looked back to find the man staring at us, a small smile turning up the corners of his mouth.

I shut the door after we exited and breathed a sigh of relief. Silas had the passenger door open and put Xander right in, shutting the door quickly so he couldn't run again. He climbed into the driver's seat.

"That man was staring as we left." I climbed into the back, setting the bags on the seat next to me. "Do we think he was just staring because of Xander or because..."

Xander was suddenly halfway over the console, growling at the bags. *"No,"* was all he communicated. No, what?

"I don't know what to think. Sometimes something completely unrelated to trauma can trigger a reaction. Maybe it was a smell or a sound." Silas tried to pull

Xander back and Xander snapped at him, turning back to the bags on the seat.

"But what if Xander was held close by here? I know he's from Washington, but he's mentioned a helicopter." I grabbed a bag and looked in it. "What is it, Xander? I don't want you to ruin your new flannels."

He snapped at the bag, and I squealed as he caught hold of it and began ripping into it. I was glad Silas hadn't started driving yet.

"Out."

"He's saying out." I tried to take the bag back from him. "You want your flannel out?"

"Bad."

"Bad?" I got the bag out of his jaws, but then Silas snatched it from me. "Hey!"

"Give me the other bags." Silas pulled forward and stopped by a dumpster. "Now, Ivy."

He jumped out and threw the bag in the open side of the dumpster and then opened my door. He took the bags from me and threw them in there too. He got back in and peeled out, not caring there were people milling about.

Xander, satisfied, sat back in the front seat. He still looked out of sorts, but wasn't shaking or growling anymore.

"It's possible that man put a tracker in one of the bags or something. Why else would he act like that?" Silas turned onto the highway and headed in the opposite direction of Arbor Falls. "Just to be on the safe side, I'm going to drive for a bit and see if anyone is following us."

"Are there people other than wolves that know about us?" There had to be *some* people. I know they went to regular schools once they were past a certain age, and with that came the possibility of regular humans knowing.

"If there are, they keep it very hush hush. The coalition would lose their shit if humans knew about us." Silas's eyes continuously darted to the mirrors as we headed west. "Which makes me wonder why my dad would want you adopted away from here. Maybe he knew you wouldn't shift."

"I've been doing a little thinking, and what if I'm half human? Maybe when I got in the accident it killed the human part of me." It sounded like something out of a book or movie, but what other explanation was there for me not shifting until that very moment. "What if it would have happened and I wasn't around other wolves? Could you imagine being a first responder and showing up to a crash site to find a wolf strapped in the driver's seat?"

He made a noncommittal noise, and the soft music that was playing made a ping. "Call Rover."

"Calling Rover." I wondered why Silas insisted on calling everyone by nicknames. Maybe it was just his thing.

The phone rang twice before it was answered. "Alpha. What's up?"

"I need to talk to Cole." Silas tapped a hand on the steering wheel. Was he nervous? He seemed nervous.

I turned in my seat and watched out the back window, trying to determine if we were being followed. There were several cars behind us and in the next lane over. They were all going about the same speed as us, but I wasn't sure what I should look for.

"Yeah? Don't tell me you did something stupid." Cole's voice was raspy with sleep, and I wondered if he'd been napping. He seemed to be more tired than usual, even though I'd healed him. But maybe I hadn't healed him completely.

Who was I kidding? There was no way my other half was human.

"I think we're being followed. There was a situation in Huntsville with Xander, and I believe whoever had him must have been there." Silas reached over and stroked Xander's head. He'd laid down in the front seat with his head on the center console.

"You aren't headed back here, are you?"

"No. I'm headed west. I'm not sure if this guy is going to try something, but for now, he appears to be alone. It's possible he tried to plant something on us to track us too." Silas switched lanes and watched the rearview mirror. "We're going to have to ditch the SUV and find another way back. Not entirely sure when and where."

"Let me talk to Sara and get back to you. Maybe you can hold him off, and Bone and Rover can come and run him off the road." Cole had a point. Those two were good at that.

I could see the car that was tailing us out the back window now. It was a black SUV with dark tinted windows, dark enough that I could only see a shadow of a man in the driver's seat.

They hung up and Silas ran a hand through his hair. "This really fucking sucks. Who are these people?"

"Maybe they're government." The man was still behind us, but keeping his distance. "The government has to know about us, right?"

"To my knowledge, no. There are a few of us on the inside to ensure that doesn't happen and the coalition to make sure wolves don't get out of hand, but I guess it's possible." He looked over at Xander. "Whatever they're doing though, they need to be taken out, and sooner rather than later."

Just another thing to pile onto the list of crazy shit. Was it always like this being a wolf? If so, I wanted a refund.

Xander whimpered, and Silas started rubbing behind his ears as he took an exit toward a residential development. I didn't know what he was doing, but he seemed to have a plan.

He turned into an apartment complex and pulled into a parking spot. The car that was tailing us didn't pull in after us, but that didn't mean he wasn't lying in wait.

"We need to get to the strip mall on the other side of this complex, and then I'll steal us a car." Silas leaned over and opened the glove compartment, pulling out a gun.

"Uh... what the fuck, Silas?" If he thought I was going to get into a stolen car, he was crazy. "Why couldn't we have just stayed on the highway and waited for Cole?"

"Bunny, do you trust me?" No, but I nodded anyway

as he turned to look at me. "Then trust that I know what I'm doing."

"What about Xander?" We got out of the SUV, keeping a close eye on our surroundings. I was suddenly freezing and wish I'd worn an extra layer. "What if he takes off again?"

Silas opened the front passenger door and Xander jumped out. "He won't. I think he's had time to process what's happening now and won't run off like that again. Right, man?"

Xander yipped once and licked at Silas's hand, then mine. Gross.

We headed toward the building in front of us, walking through the breezeway and out the other side where more buildings were. We were headed toward the back of the complex where a fence backed up to a strip mall.

"I've never climbed a fence before." We were speed walking, and Silas shoved the gun in the back of his pants. "How is Xander going to get over? Are you going to throw him?"

"No. Wolves can jump." He texted someone, I was guessing Rover, and then shoved his phone in his pocket.

This whole thing was a bad idea.

"You go first." Silas was watching behind us. "Run and then jump as high as you can."

I didn't know what the hell I was doing, but I surged forward, the fence looming ahead. My feet pounded across the ground, and I jumped before I reached the fence. I grabbed onto the top bar and used my feet to climb so I could pull myself up and over.

I landed safely on the other side and waited impatiently for Silas and Xander. Silas knelt a few feet out from the fence and Xander ran and jumped onto his back while Silas stood, giving him an extra boost.

Wolves must practice that kind of maneuver because they worked in tandem so well I would have never known they barely knew each other.

Silas practically flew over the fence after Xander, and then we were running along the back of the strip mall. What we were doing was crazy, but what other choice did we have?

"Are we absolutely, one hundred percent certain that man was following us?" We rounded the side of the building and slowed to a walk, Xander between us like a companion dog. "Maybe it was just one of those instances of heading to the same place at the same time."

"Bad man." Xander looked up at me with glossy eyes.

I didn't understand why he was speaking like he couldn't get the words out, but I missed the Xander who had emerged over the past several days.

"Better safe than sorry." Silas was focused straight ahead, and before I could protest, he'd climbed into an idling delivery truck. "Let's go."

"You've got to be kidding me." I had no choice but to climb in after them. Was this how packages always went missing? Stolen delivery trucks?

Silas pulled out of the parking lot and handed me

his phone. "Tell me where to go. Rover was sending me a rendezvous point."

Shaking my head because now he was trying to sound like some big shot secret agent, I opened the text and pulled up the address on maps. "I'm dreaming, right? Or this is some initiation prank for me to be accepted into your pack?"

"Which way do I need to go, Ivy?" Silas wasn't messing around.

"Head east, back the way we came. On the edge of Huntsville is a strip club." I really wanted to throw the phone because this entire day was a disaster.

Couldn't I just have one day where nothing went wrong? Had I done something to bring me bad karma?

"Oh, *Naked Goddess*?"

"Yes." I sighed. "Of course you know exactly where the strip club is."

"Hey, I'm a man that appreciates a woman's form. I can't wait to see you strip for me one of these days." Silas glanced over at me and gave me a goofy grin. "I can install a stripper pole, if you want."

Shaking my head, I patted my leg for Xander. He made a sound that sounded an awful lot like a grumble and then put his head on my thigh. "I don't really know how to act with him like this."

"What you're doing is fine. We don't normally interact with each other like this, but it feels good to be pet. I see why dogs are fans of it."

A comfortable silence fell over us and we rode in silence about fifteen minutes before Silas pulled off the highway and into the strip club parking lot. There was an SUV and a truck waiting, and we quickly piled into the SUV.

Cole and Eli were inside, and I threw myself at them, letting them fuss over me. I'd been trying to keep my cool for Xander's sake, but now that we were safe, I was shaking.

I had the horrible feeling that we'd escaped for now, but would see that man again.

CHAPTER EIGHTEEN

Cole

Xander was on the couch, his head in Ivy's lap as she stroked between his eyes. It had been hours since we got them back to Silas's den, but he was still in his wolf form. With him not communicating, we had a difficult time deciding what to do.

Silas had switched vehicles again at another stop and gone back with his betas to see if they could locate the man but had turned up with nothing. They also circled back to where they had thrown out the bags of clothing and searched through them. There was nothing but clothes inside.

Xander had been through extreme trauma, a lot we still weren't aware of. His current lack of communication made me wonder if he hadn't hallucinated the whole thing. Him freaking out might have then affected Silas's and Ivy's judgment of the situation.

But it was better to err on the side of caution.

I sure hadn't, and look what had happened.

I felt like a failure. I couldn't protect my mate, my pack, or myself. Everything my father built and worked hard to cultivate was gone. The pack would never be the same, even if I got my spot as alpha back.

How do you trust an alpha to protect your very essence when he can't even sniff out his own beta plotting against him?

Sara estimated he'd been plotting for at least three months based on internet searches, vehicle locations, and tones used in communications with me and the other betas. It was easy to miss when you weren't monitoring every move someone in the pack made. But maybe I would have if I'd heeded my father's advice all those years ago.

And now there was a possible threat nearby, and the pack was vulnerable without me at the lead. I was so disappointed in myself I could hardly bear it.

"Cole, did you hear me?" Eli asked, concern in his voice.

"What?" I looked up from the spot I was staring at on the coffee table. There was the faintest ring from a cup that had needed a coaster.

"Is this movie okay? Xander likes action movies." He gestured to the projector screen. "Maybe it will help bring him back."

I stood, stretching and faking a yawn. "I think I'm going to head to bed."

"It's barely eight, old man." Silas threw a piece of popcorn at me, and I let out a half-hearted growl. If I were in the mood to fight, I'd have taken the bowl and dumped it on his head.

"It's been a long day. The other pack will hopefully be here tomorrow, so I need to get some sleep." Before anyone could stop me, I walked toward the hall with the bunk rooms.

I hated to admit it, but I liked the setup Silas had, which allowed any of the pack members to stay in the den. A few did often, but most had homes throughout the territory. Silas even had a house; he just chose not to stay in it for whatever reason. It was pretty far away from anyone else, but it was where he grew up.

After getting ready for bed, I went into the room we'd taken over as our own. We had moved three of the twin mattresses onto the floor to make a giant bed. We could have slept in separate beds, but what was the fun in that?

I didn't realize how well I'd sleep in a group until we tried it the night before. It brought a level of comfort that sleeping alone or even with just Ivy didn't bring. They were my family now. My own little pack.

And as much as I hated to admit it, Silas was part of that.

I laid down and shut my eyes, hoping sleep would take me fast. I'd not gotten a lot of sleep the night before, but my mind raced with thoughts about what-ifs.

What if Dante beats me when we go head-to-head?
What if Ivy is hurt?

What if there are people doing horrible things to our kind?

The door opened, and I knew who it was without opening my eyes. Her scent was one of my favorite things in the world, and I was just realizing it.

"Are you asleep?" The mattress dipped as she laid behind me, her hand sliding over my back and around to rest on my stomach.

"Not yet." How could I sleep when there were so many things on my mind?

"You've been quiet all day. I'm worried about you." She moved a leg between mine, and I sighed. "You're sad."

"I'm not sad." I put my hand over hers to stop her from stroking along my scar. It was too much of a reminder of my failure. "I'm just... disappointed."

"In me?" She tensed behind me but didn't pull away.

"No. In myself." My voice was barely a whisper. "I failed."

She was quiet, and I thought maybe she'd fallen asleep, but then she kissed my wolf tattoo. "You didn't fail. You were ambushed, Cole. No one could have guessed he would stoop that low and do such heinous things to take the pack away from you." She moved the hand from my stomach and began tracing my back tattoo.

"My father warned me years ago that if anyone challenged me, I had to take them out. I thought Dante was just running his mouth with his toxic masculinity bullshit." I shook my head, not believing I could be so foolish. "This is on me, Ivy, as much as it's on him.

Three lives are lost because of my pride. I thought everyone in the pack was satisfied with me as alpha. I didn't think anyone would dare challenge me or stab me in the back. But he did, and I almost lost everything."

"It's going to be all right, Cole. We're going to get your pack back." She kissed the center of my back and moved her hand to my arm where she ran a finger up and down the muscle. "Maybe the two packs can even become one again. Stronger together."

I snorted. "When hell freezes over."

"Hell is a place that does actually freeze over." She laughed and then grew quiet for a minute. "We need to find out what really happened to Xander and his pack."

I rolled to my back, and she ended up sprawled halfway on my chest. "We will. If anything would have happened to you today, I..."

My eyes watered. Fuck. I was more fucked up than I thought.

"I'm fine, Cole." She took my hand and put it over her heart. "I feel like all of this... turmoil is happening because of me."

"Don't. None of this is on you. You barely got here." I pushed her hair behind her ear. I loved when she wore it down. "This has been brewing for a long time, and as for Xander... how many other wolves have suffered like he has but not made it out of wherever they were?"

A tear slid down her cheek, and I caught it with my thumb. My entire body ached with the need to make sure she was safe and happy. So far, I was doing a horrible job of it.

"We have to stop them," she whispered.

"We will. I promise you, we will do everything in our power to stop them from hurting any more of us." I moved my hand to the back of her head and pulled her toward me, pressing my forehead to hers. "I'm glad that we all have each other, as much as I don't care for sharing you."

She smiled. "Ah, so now he doesn't mind. Could it be because you like the sexy times?"

"Do I like seeing my woman get off? Hell, yes." I brushed my lips over hers. "I guess if I'm not the one doing it, it's almost just as good watching it happen with a front-row seat."

She moved on top of me, straddling my waist, her heat scorching the bare skin right above the top of my boxers. "You like to watch?"

My hands went to her thighs, and I wished leggings weren't covering them. Would she be pissed if I just ripped them right off her?

"I like to participate." My thumbs slipped to her inner thighs, squeezing her legs possessively. I needed her. "Why don't you slide back a little farther so you can feel just how much I want to participate."

"Mm..." Her fingers glided across my chest, circling my nipples. "How about I slide up?"

Fuck, she was a force I didn't know how to handle. She stood, stripping out of her clothes, baring herself to me. Pulling my cock out of my boxers, I stroked myself as she spread her pussy lips and showed me just how much she wanted me.

"Jesus, Ivy. Fucking sit on my face and let me taste that gorgeous cunt, or I'm going to throw you down on this mattress and take what's mine." I was holding on by a thread with the view I had.

She walked forward and lowered herself so she was straddling my face. Her scent hit me, and I groaned, using my thumbs to open her to me.

With the first flick of my tongue, her hands went to my hair. With the second, she gasped and relaxed. I licked, sucked, and nipped her cunt, my tongue making its way to her entrance.

"Cole, yes. Please, I need..." Her hips moved in small thrusts, urging me to fuck her with my tongue.

I pushed just the tip inside of her and used my thumb to rub her clit in circles. My cock ached at the thought of burying myself deep. She was already soaked and ready to take me, but I was greedy and wanted her clawing at me to take her.

"Oh fuck, please." She was begging for it, her legs trembling as I teased her hole with the tip of my tongue a little deeper each time.

I pulled away, kissing her inner thigh. She let out a helpless cry, and one of her hands left my hair to take care of herself. I took her wrist and sucked two of her fingers into my mouth.

"What do you want?" My voice was low and teasing. "Do you want to come? Is that what you want?"

Her breaths were coming in pants as I took her hand and guided it to her pussy. She whimpered as I joined one of her fingers with two of mine and pushed into her. "Cole…"

"Do you feel how wet you are for me? Fucking perfect." I bent our fingers as we slid out, brushing over the button of nerves that had her gasping. I added another one of her fingers and pushed in again. "Wet enough to take two cocks. Have you ever had two cocks buried inside you, Ivy?"

I must have left her speechless because all she could do was moan. My dick was hard enough to forge a sword, and my hips moved, trying to seek relief.

"I'm going to take our fingers out, and you're going to ride my cock, baby. Ride it hard and don't stop until we're both fucking coming."

She was on the edge of snapping as I removed our fingers, moving them upward to brush over her throbbing clit. She wasted no time sliding down my body, eyes locked on mine as I licked my fingers clean.

Her cunt enveloped my cock, and I gripped the sheets, the feel of her surrounding me almost too much. "Ride me."

And fucking ride me she did.

Her tits bounced as she took me over and over, sliding up and down my cock like I was her ride or die. I sat up, my abs protesting from lack of use, and took a nipple between my teeth.

Her pussy clenched around me as she worked her clit against my pelvis, throwing her head back as pleasure overtook her. She was loud, and I knew they could probably hear us out in the den, but I didn't give a fuck. Let them hear how hard I made my mate come.

Her thrusts slowed, and I maneuvered her to her back, pushing her legs wide. "Grab onto the back of your legs."

"Bossy." Bossy, but she listened and grabbed on, holding herself wide open for me to bury myself in her heat.

My balls tingled as I neared my orgasm, and I leaned forward and took her mouth, our tongues tangling as I slid home one last time before exploding inside of her.

Burying my face in her neck, I circled my hips, buried to my hilt, letting her milk every drop from me.

She'd taken not just my pleasure, but my entire being. And that included my heart.

∼

NOT LONG AFTER CLEANING UP, Xander and Eli came into the room and took the other two spots on our makeshift giant mattress. Xander was still in his wolf form and curled in a ball between Eli and Ivy. Nothing seemed to work to get through to him.

At least he wasn't trying to attack any of us like he did the first time we met.

Seeing what his captors had done to him mentally just made me even more aware of what could have happened with their little trip into Huntsville. I had known it was a bad idea for Ivy to go with Silas but had let her anyway.

Listen to you, you sound like a douche.

The sounds of them sleeping safely next to me did

nothing to ease the inner voice that wouldn't shut up. I got up carefully and slipped out of the room.

The den was bathed in darkness besides a string of LED lights hung around the front door. I walked past the sectionals where Silas was sleeping curled up with some pillows.

How was I going to handle seeing Ivy cuddled up next to him or him buried inside her?

Clenching my fists, I turned toward my destination: the kitchen. There was nothing a late-night snack couldn't fix.

I opened the industrial-size refrigerator and grabbed the whole rotisserie chicken that was sitting there calling my name. We had raging metabolisms, so there was always food around.

Shutting the door with my hip, I nearly dropped the container when I came face to face with Silas. He was rubbing one of his eyes with his palm, his other eye locked on the chicken in my hands.

"That's my chicken."

For fuck's sake. Were we really going to do this in the middle of the night over a damn chicken?

"Where's your name?" I examined it as I walked to the counter. "Hm. Don't see *bitch ass motherfucker* written anywhere on it, so I guess it's mine now."

He reached for it, and I held it to the side, away from his grasp. He grumbled something and went to the refrigerator, digging inside and pulling out a container.

As soon as he opened the lid, I licked my lips and tried to look inside. "What is that?"

"Bacon wrapped sausage. No. You can't have any because you won't share my chicken." He hopped up on the metal counter and pulled a piece out.

"You're just going to eat it cold?" I opened the chicken and ripped off a leg. "What kind of sausage?"

"Wouldn't you like to know?"

I pushed the chicken over to him before hopping up on the counter. We used to get in a lot of trouble when we were kids for eating on the counter. I smiled at the memory of my mom yelling at us for the hundredth time.

"What happened to us?" I bit into my chicken. "Why did we let our fathers ruin our friendship?"

Silas handed me his container. "Hell if I know. They were our fathers. What were we supposed to do at eight years old?"

"We've been adults for a long time. We could have… talked." I was just as much to blame for the gaping hole between us as he was. But I had tried, even if half-heartedly.

"And let you keep accusing my father of the unthinkable? No thanks." He shook his head and leaned over to grab a fork and knife out of a drawer. "But I guess now we have to."

"Yeah." I bit into a sausage and groaned. "Fuck, these are good."

"As good as whatever you and Ivy did earlier?" He didn't look up at me but was smiling as he cut into the chicken. "The sounds echo."

I should have been embarrassed, but it just made me puff out my chest. "Nothing is better than her."

"So, what now? We just pretend we haven't been dipshits for the last twenty-six years?" He snorted.

"I still don't trust you or your pack. As soon as this is over, your betas are getting an ass kicking. I've been trying to keep my cool around them because we need your help, but they almost killed Ivy." It took every ounce of my willpower not to shift and show them who they fucking ran off the road. "They also owe me a car."

"I kicked their asses the night they came back and told me they caused you to crash. I would have demoted them from their positions, but it's slim pickings in my pack. Seems all the strong, intelligent ones are in your pack."

"Maybe they just need a strong alpha to lead them." *Nice one, Cole. Way to reconcile.*

Silas stopped chewing and narrowed his eyes. I probably should have been more careful with my words considering he had a steak knife on the counter next to him. Instead of stabbing me, he shrugged.

"You're probably right. I didn't even want to be alpha if I'm being honest. Maybe if I would have had more time to train and learn from my father, things would be different."

Maybe, or maybe he would have been strong enough to beat me, just like Dante had.

CHAPTER NINETEEN

Ivy

I woke up feeling well-rested and like I could take on the world. My feet were toasty from Xander lying on them and I slid them out from underneath him, trying not to wake him up. I stood and stretched; my body was slightly sore from my activities the night before.

Xander let out a whimper, and his paws moved in his sleep like he was running. He went from a whimper to a growl and then jumped up so fast I nearly fell backward, my feet unsteady on the mattress.

"Xander!"

He turned to face me, a blood curdling snarl making me want to shift and put him in his place. I held my hands at my sides and backed up a step. He stalked forward.

Was he just messing around? The look in his eyes told me no.

"Xander, it's me, Ivy. Your mate." I repeated it through our connection, hoping he'd snap out of it.

"Mate?" He sounded confused, but at least had responded. *"Ivy?"*

"Yes. Come back to me, Xander." I knelt, risking my face so I'd be at his level. *"You're safe now. We're all safe."*

I didn't know that for sure, but his wolf keeping him locked inside was dangerous for the human part of him. If wolf therapists existed, we needed to find him one. I probably needed to find myself one too.

He cocked his head to the side, and then he shifted on his hands and knees. His head was down, and he was panting as if he had just run a mile at his fastest pace.

"Xander, are you okay?" I itched to reach out and touch him but didn't want to spook him.

"Ivy?" His voice was strained and gravelly. "What... How?"

I didn't quite understand what he was asking me, and I tentatively reached out my hand to touch his that was gripping a pillow. "We're still at Silas's den. Your wolf kind of took over, didn't he?"

He lifted his head, and his green eyes met mine. "He... I smelled him." He sat back on his ass. "He was there, in Huntsville. I think he was alone."

"Who's he? Is it one of the people that had you?" I crawled across the mattress and wrapped my arms around him, putting my head against his chest.

"Yes." His shaky arms wrapped around me, his

fingers clutching onto my shirt. "You have to believe me."

He must have been listening when we talked about whether it was a hallucination. As much as I wanted to believe him, it was looking less likely the man had been anything other than that… a man. Sara was going to go through security footage to try to identify him.

"Maybe he was there on vacation." I hated to think there was a facility that tortured and experimented on wolf shifters right in our backyard.

A loud bang and shouts came through the door and caused both of us to jump. Xander's eyes widened, but luckily, he didn't shift back into his wolf. We had talked the night before about being careful about noise for the sake of Xander.

"What the hell?" I jumped up and rushed to the door, opening it just in time to hear Silas yelling.

"I'm not going to let you go and fucking die. Fuck that asshole."

By the time I made it down the hall, Silas had Cole by the front of the shirt shoved against the wall by the door. Both men were red in the face, but Cole wasn't fighting back. I felt like I could never leave those two alone in a room together without them going at it.

Eli was sitting at the dining table with his face in his hands, and Sara was next to him, staring at the laptop screen. What the hell had happened?

"It's none of your business what I do. What choice do I have left?" Cole shoved Silas off him and fixed his shirt.

I'd seen enough. "What the hell's going on out here?"

Silas threw his hands in the air and marched over to the table, spinning the laptop so I could see the screen as I approached it. "Cole wants to go on a suicide mission."

"What am I looking at?" On the screen was a video with a still of the wolf mural inside the den at Cole's.

Silas reached around the laptop and pressed the play button. At first, it stayed focused on the mural, but then it panned out to show at least twenty people bound and gagged, fear in their eyes. A few were even shifted, shredded clothes spread out around them.

"What the fuck?" My eyes welled with tears, and Xander came up behind me and put his hand on my lower back. It did little to comfort me from what I was watching.

"Cole. I really wished it didn't have to come to this, but you see, you need to pay for what you've done." Whoever was filming backed up, bringing Dante into view. "Do you see these traitors here?" He waved a gun, gesturing to the hostages. "They've decided not to believe I'm the alpha now. They've made their beds. The question is, are you going to let them lie in them too?"

He walked in front of the group and stopped in front of a teenage boy. I held my breath, hoping he wasn't about to kill him.

"Will you just have Ivy's blood on your hands? Or will you have these wolves' blood too?" He shoved the gun under the boy's chin, making his head tilt back at an unnatural angle. "You have four hours after I see that you've watched this video. Or else."

He kicked the boy, making him fall over, and fired the gun at the mural, hitting the wolf in the forehead. The video stopped, and I was left staring at the mural again. Was Cole really that big of a threat to Dante that he would kill twenty people?

I finally looked up, my attention immediately going to Cole. He was pacing back and forth, his hands in his hair. "He really is still trying to pass me off as dead? What about that guy from the fire station?"

"He was one of the hostages." Cole pinched the bridge of his nose. "Fuck. Fuck!"

Was there wolf protocol for something like this? We couldn't just call the police to come in with their tactical unit. There were way too many variables involved; like the fact we shifted when in danger.

"What's the plan?" I managed to ask without my voice shaking, but my body certainly was.

Silas slammed the screen of the laptop closed. "I can tell you what it's fucking not. It's not turning yourself over to that fucking psychopath and dying."

Cole and Silas were in each other's faces again, and Cole's hands balled into fists. "It's not your decision. Sometimes we have to sacrifice one for the many."

"You. Aren't. Doing. It." Silas was barely holding onto his control as he bit out the words.

"Guys, let's-" I needed to defuse the tension, not just for Xander's sake, but for all of ours. Eli was still sitting with his face in his hands, and Sara looked like she was ready to burst into tears.

"It's not your life. He wants me, and he's not going to stop at just twenty. He'll keep going until I turn myself over to him." Cole backed away, looking defeated. "This is the only way, Silas. You know it is, you just don't want to admit I'm right."

I started to move toward him, but Xander wrapped an arm around my waist, stopping me. He shook his head when I looked at him in protest.

"Then I'll go with you," Silas said firmly.

"Fuck that. I won't let you die because of my mistakes." He went for the door and Silas headed him off. "Move, Silas."

"No." Silas stood tall, his chest puffed out and eyes blazing. "You go, we both go, Coco."

A tear slid down Cole's cheek and Silas grabbed him by the back of the neck, bringing their foreheads together. The room was quiet as they had their moment together.

We sat down at the table, and Xander reached his hand across the table to Eli. Eli had finally removed his hands from his head, and his face was splotchy from his tears.

Eli gave his hand a quick squeeze. "I'm glad to see you're back."

"How long ago did you watch the video?" I took Xander's other hand, hoping if both of us held onto him, he would stay with us.

Cole and Silas hugged, slapping each other's backs, and came to join us. Cole sat to my right and gave me a sad smile. God, I hated seeing him like that.

"It was sent about an hour ago, and we opened it

about twenty minutes ago." Sara pulled the laptop back toward her. "We have a lot of emails from pack members unwilling to follow Dante's deranged ideas. He had a pack meeting last night and called for wolves to take their rightful place in the world."

"We have numbers on our side, right? Let's just storm in there and kill him." It seemed easy enough of a plan. I wasn't a violent person usually, but something about Dante made me want to draw blood.

"He has twenty hostages. We can't risk all those lives." Cole tapped his knuckles on the table. "We're just going to have to call the coalition for help, or I'm going to have to turn myself over."

Silas groaned. "I know they're going to catch wind of it all eventually, but who knows what the outcome will be if they're involved. You remember what happened with the Woodford pack about five years ago, right? They made them all split up into different packs."

"We aren't running a wolf fighting ring, Silas." Cole was restless in his seat. "But you're right. They don't like attention drawn to our kind, and who knows what will happen if twenty people suddenly go missing... Plus, we have Ivy to think of."

"What is this coalition exactly?" They kept mentioning it in conversations, and it was making me nervous. It didn't sound like they were tolerant of anything outside of the norm, and I certainly fit that profile.

"They make major decisions about packs that threaten to expose us. They always send messengers with their decisions or do it via email to keep their identities a secret." Sara opened the laptop.

"I know this is going to sound crazy, but I think we can pull off a rescue if we lure Dante away from the den." Xander squeezed my hand. "It sounds like he has everyone believing Ivy is dead. What better way to throw him off his game than to have her show up? He'll be so worried about her exposing his lies, he'll get sloppy, right?"

"Absolutely not." Cole stood and began pacing. "I won't put her at risk."

"He has a point. It's only a matter of time before he comes after me again, anyway. He knows I'm stronger than him. I proved it the last time I went head-to-head with him and sent him running with his tail tucked." I stood and went to Cole. "I can lure him away so you guys can get control of the situation in the den."

"Ivy…" Cole frowned and ran a hand down his face. "If he knows he can't beat you in wolf form, he knows he can beat you with a bullet."

"If I catch him unaware, I can shoot him with an arrow."

"You've only shot that thing a few times and never at a living target. Shooting a human is way different than shooting a ceramic rabbit. We don't know if it was just a fluke or…" I put my finger against his lips.

"I feel it in my soul, and I know that doesn't help ease the worry, but trust me. I was born to shoot a bow and arrow." I kissed him quickly and turned to the others. "I can use the treehouse and we can make sure he knows I'm in the territory."

"No." Cole was shaking his head vehemently.

"We just need to figure out a way to get him away from the den and to where I am. With backup, of course." It sounded like it would work to me. "Eli, what do you think?"

Eli had been silent, his eyes ping-ponging as the discussion happened. I could tell he was thinking it through.

"I think with Dante away from his followers, it will give Cole and Silas a fighting chance to put them on their backs. With Dante there, they'll be less likely to surrender." Eli gave me a sad smile. "As scared as I am, I think Ivy's right."

A calmness washed over me. I could do this. I had to.

∼

It felt like we were going to war, and I guess in a way we were. I'd raided Carly's closet and chose brown tones to blend in with the tree trunks in the forest. My hair was pulled back in a braid, and I pulled a beanie on over it. I didn't plan on shifting since my best weapon at taking down a gun wielding asshole was a bow and arrow.

I was embracing my inner huntress, except this was real life and not some dystopian blood bath.

"Are you sure you want to do this?" Cole adjusted the strap of my quiver of arrows and left his hand on my shoulder. "Because you don't have to."

"You're my family now. I protect my family." I

leaned forward and kissed him. "Bone, Rover, and Eli will be with me too."

"I know, but… it's dangerous." He pulled me into a hug. "As soon as we free the hostages, we'll be right there. Don't do anything you'll regret."

We'd talked at length about what killing a person would mean for me. There was, of course, the whole thing about being a murderer, but also the emotional toll it would bring. It needed to be done, though. What other option did we have?

There were no other options.

"I just wish the reinforcements were here. Damn weather." The same weather system had hit the Tahoe pack, and it left them much worse off without power and buried in four feet of snow. In March.

"They'll be here in a few hours, but we don't have that much time." Cole gave me one last kiss and went to join Silas, Manny, and several other WAP members.

"This is a good idea, right?" I kept my voice low so Cole and Silas wouldn't hear me.

"We'll be right there with guns to back you up." Bone shoved some ammo in his pocket. "I'm a really good shot."

Rover nodded but was quiet. He looked nervous, and that was the last thing we needed.

"Eli?" I watched him as he put ammo in a gun and then slipped it into a holster. "You can stay here if you have any doubts."

"Nope. We're in this together. I might be the omega, but that doesn't mean I don't know how to fight." He looked over my shoulder. "We'll give you guys a few minutes." The three of them walked out of the barn to wait for me.

I turned to find Silas coming my way. He took my hand. "Bunny, before you go…" He pulled me to him, my hand going to his chest, and captured my mouth in a searing kiss.

I leaned into him, letting myself have this moment. I refused to think it could be both our first and last kiss, but the possibility was there. We weren't trained for what we were going to face, and any number of things could go wrong.

"There's more where that came from," he murmured, pulling away and cupping my cheek. "Be safe."

"I will."

He left me breathless, watching as he walked out with Cole and the others.

It was showtime.

CHAPTER TWENTY

Ivy

We rode in Bone's truck in silence, two ATVs loaded in the back. Bone turned off the highway, and we were on our way into the EAP's territory. It was mid-morning, and most people were probably at work or staying clear of Dante. We saw no one at the four houses we passed.

Pulling to a stop at the end of the road, we unloaded the ATVs and rode through the forest, hoping to avoid any patrols that would stop us or slow us down. Either Dante didn't think we'd come through the forest, or he really didn't have that many on his side. I hoped it was the latter.

Eli slowed down as we approached where the treehouse was and then came to a complete stop and sniffed the air. "Something's wrong."

It smelled like burned wood, and my stomach dropped. We continued at a slower pace, Bone and Rover right behind us.

The large tree the treehouse had been built around was still standing, but the entire top half of it was burned, the remnants of the treehouse scattered around the base of the tree.

"It's okay." Eli didn't sound too convincing as we circled back and parked the ATVs behind a large crop of bushes. "It was just a treehouse."

"How did he know?" I jumped off and made sure my bow and arrows were easily accessible. "Maybe he's always known it was there."

"He probably smelled us when he tried to find us." Eli left the key in the ignition and gave me a sad smile. "We can build a new, better one now."

"Yeah, but…" I turned to Rover and Bone because now was not the time to worry about the treehouse. "So, new plan. We'll have to hide behind trees. I guess that's better than nothing."

"You ready?" Bone took out the phone Sara had given him and pulled up Cole's Instagram.

"As ready as I'm going to be." I took the phone from him and pushed the button to start the live feed. Bone had already published a post that Sara had set up that tagged all the wolves we knew were involved with Dante.

I only had to wait a few minutes for people to join the live feed.

"Hi. I'm here today to tell you the story of a jealous little boy who couldn't make it to the top without lying and deceiving those he was supposed to protect." I watched as the number of watchers increased. "You're probably wondering what the hell is going on. Is this pre-recorded? Am I seeing a ghost?"

Dante's Instagram handle joined the feed, and I grinned. I showed enough of what was behind me for him to recognize the location, which was infinitely easier now with the treehouse destroyed.

"I'm not a ghost. I'm alive and well. In fact, I'm right here in the forest. I see our guest of honor has arrived! Dante, care to tell them what you did?"

I wished I could see his face. I just hoped he was angry enough to come after me and not hurt the hostages.

The comments went nuts, and I couldn't keep up with them. "It's time for me to take my place as alpha."

I turned off the phone and handed it back to Bone, who was grinning from ear to ear. "That probably really pissed him off."

"What if he doesn't show?" I looked around for a good place to hide. The plan had been to fire at him from inside the safety of the treehouse with Bone, Rover, and Eli hiding around the area as backup.

"He will. He wanted you dead because you could take him. Now that you've called him out on his lies and challenged him, he won't be able to stop himself." Eli gave me a quick kiss and pointed to a large tree. "You're going to have to be extra careful now that you won't have the coverage of the treehouse."

"Text just came through from Silas. They have eyes

on him and two others leaving the den and heading this way."

It worked. It actually fucking worked.

Nerves took over me, and I shook my hands in front of me. "What if I can't hit him or he shoots me?"

"I'll draw his attention to me." Eli started to move away, and I grabbed his arm.

"That's not what we discussed!" Panic welled up inside me and I gasped for air. "Oh my God, what if he has an automatic rifle?"

This wasn't some video game where I'd have health regeneration or a reset button. There was a possibility someone might die.

"Look at me." Eli touched my cheek, and I met his brown eyes that were molten with concern. "We can jump on the quads and go. He left the den. That was the goal."

I sucked in a breath. "No. We have a chance to take care of him for good."

He started to speak again, but the sounds of off-road vehicles came from the direction Dante would be coming from. Just as we expected, he wasn't going to shift because he was armed.

We separated, me hiding behind a tree and the other three spreading out. I felt sick to my stomach but had no choice now but to follow through with what I'd set out to do.

I pulled an arrow from my quiver and got it ready.

They came to a stop right where we had been gathered. Our scent was strongest there, but then we'd split.

"Come out here and fight me!" he bellowed, his voice echoing in the forest. "Get him!"

Eli, what are you doing?

They weren't firing their guns yet, and I shut my eyes. *You can do this, Ivy.*

I moved out from behind the tree at the same time Dante turned. I lifted my bow and fired.

The arrow sliced through the air, landing right where I intended. He screamed as blood blossomed from his crotch. I stalked forward; another arrow ready to go. Shots were fired not far away. *Please be safe.*

"You fucking bitch! I should have shot you in the head!" His words were laced with pain and he reached behind him.

I let the next arrow go, aiming for his arm. He bellowed, the gun he was reaching for falling to the ground. He dropped to his knees, yanking the arrow out of his forearm and then yanking the one from his groin. A feral growl left him, and he shifted, ripping the arrow from his shoulder.

Fuck. I couldn't shoot an animal.

What the hell was I even thinking? I'd just shot a man in the dick.

With whatever strength he had left, he jumped forward. I released my last arrow, straight for his chest. His yelp hurt my heart, and he fell to the ground, the arrow pushing deeper as he landed.

Rolling onto his back, he howled the most pitiful sound I'd ever heard. A part of me, for whatever reason, mourned the loss of a pack member.

But he'd tranquilized me.

Bound me.

Muzzled me.

Threw me in the river to die.

Harmed my mates.

I approached cautiously, ready to shift if needed. He stared up at me, tears soaking the hair around his eyes. "Shift," I commanded.

He whimpered and then shifted, hair still covering his arms in patches. He gritted his teeth, which were bloody. His hands went to the arrow in his chest. Gurgles came out as he tried to speak.

"You don't deserve to die with the honor of being in your wolf form." I wasn't sure what moved me to say those words, but they felt truer than anything I'd ever said. "Things could have been different, Dante."

Footfalls came from behind me, but I didn't look over my shoulder.

Dante reached out and grabbed onto my ankle. "I... will... haunt... you..."

Kicking his hand away, I backed up as Eli went for his neck to deal his final blow. I turned, not wanting to see the aftermath.

"We're coming." Cole's voice was all I needed to lose the last bit of composure I had.

Tears streamed down my cheeks as I looked out at the forest. Bone and Rover had the two men that had been with Dante on the ground, guns trained on them to keep them from moving. One man had blood coming from his leg.

I gasped, somehow hearing the last breath leave Dante's body. Falling to my knees, I clutched my chest.

What the hell was happening? It felt like my heart was being pumped full of blood and was going to burst. Was I having a heart attack?

My body didn't feel like my own and then my wolf burst free, the sounds of ripping fabric and my growl startling me.

Power coursed through my body, and I tilted my head back and let out a howl like I'd never heard before. Other howls sounded around me. The men on the ground and Bone and Rover had shifted.

"Ivy?" I turned to find Eli down on his belly, his eyes wide as he stared up at me. *"Your eyes."*

What about my eyes?

I was like an outsider, watching as my wolf took over. I approached Eli, my teeth bared. This was *not* what I wanted.

The words that were sent through our connection were buried deep inside me, as if they were preloaded for this moment. I spoke in a foreign language, a question at the end, but the power in them nearly brought me to my knees.

Eli whimpered and rolled over, baring his neck to me. I lunged forward, biting him, the tang of his blood sending a surge of power and desire through me.

I turned, finding Xander had arrived, already lying on his back, baring his neck. He watched me with an intensity that sent a chill down my spine. I repeated the foreign words to him. I didn't even wait since he was already ready for me. I bit into his neck, the power inside growing.

Silas and Cole stood next to each other, looking on

with teeth bared. I growled right back, moving toward them, my hair bristling as they continued to stand their ground.

"*Submit.*" My growl was savage.

Silas made a final growl and then lowered to the ground. I repeated the same thing to him as I did to the other two and he rolled onto his back, giving me his neck.

"*Cole.*" Was I going to have to fight him? I really didn't want to. Something told me whatever was happening was beyond our wolves, and I would win.

Cole's growls stopped, and we stared at each other for a moment before he lowered to the ground, completing whatever had just happened.

Mine.

The wind swirled around us, howls filling the sky as the other members of the pack, including Silas's pack, howled. They were acknowledging me as their alpha.

"*What the hell just happened?*" Silas cocked his head to the side. "*And have your eyes always glowed silver?*"

"*What? They're glowing?*" Whatever had come over me seemed to have passed, and I had control of my wolf again.

Cole nuzzled my neck. "*Glowing like you're a superhero.*"

The other three gathered around to nuzzle me and my heart soared. I loved these men. They were it for me.

"*I hate to break this little party up, but we need to take care of the body and clean up the treehouse. I'm surprised it didn't catch the whole forest on fire. It's saturated with kerosene."* Hearing Manny in my head was something I'd have to get used to.

"I don't understand why he'd burn the treehouse." Eli was wistful. *"We had so many good memories there."*

"Wait, how can you speak to me?" Manny cocked his head to the side. I knew eventually I wouldn't find it adorable anymore when another wolf did it, but for now, it was still cute to see a wolf with a curious tilt to the head.

"I don't know. I can hear everyone." Eli looked at me, then at Cole as if he had all the answers.

"I can hear everyone too. It's like a group chat." Xander let out a yip. *"Does that mean..."*

"We're all alphas?" Xander, Silas, Cole, and Eli all said it at the same time.

"Ivy's the alpha." Manny backed up a step. *"What the hell is going on?"*

I didn't have an answer for that. We were all safe, and right then, that was all that mattered.

CHAPTER TWENTY-ONE

Ivy

I was the alpha.

How did that even happen? I didn't know what the hell I was doing and was much more likely to bite someone's head off than Cole or Silas. There wasn't an alpha bone in my body... except there was.

Which was why I was lying awake at two in the morning instead of sleeping. *I was born to be an alpha.* My father had been the alpha, and who the hell knew what my mother had been.

The week had been insane. After the stunt Dante pulled, then my wolf naming herself alpha of both packs, people were up in arms. I couldn't blame them.

I scooted out of bed, careful not to wake Cole. He'd been quiet in the last week, offering me advice but not fighting what had happened, at least not yet. I'd tried to talk to him about his feelings, but he had shrugged and shut down.

He'd been groomed to be an alpha, and I'd swooped in and taken that away. I might have been his mate, but that didn't change the fact that I had the job.

Job.

I needed to decide what to do about my career. With Cole and Silas as my pseudo co-alphas, I could probably swing at least part-time. But was that what I wanted?

No wonder I couldn't sleep.

I shut the bedroom door quietly and tiptoed down the stairs. Our massive custom-made bed that everyone laughs about on the internet wouldn't arrive for a few more weeks, so for the time being, I was bed hopping.

Jokingly, I'd put a sign-up sheet on the refrigerator, and I damn near had to break up a fight between Cole and Silas. Pulling two grown-ass men apart for fighting over a pen was not how I thought cohabitating would go.

The faint sounds of talking and flickering lights from the television came from downstairs. I got to the bottom and stood behind the couch, where Silas was sitting.

"What are you doing up?" I wrapped my arms around him and kissed his cheek.

He grabbed onto my arm as I started to pull away and turned his head to take my lips. We had yet to do anything besides kiss, but that was mainly my fault for passing out every night as soon as I hit the pillows.

Only, I had too much weighing on me.

And an ache between my legs. There was definitely that too.

"I should be asking you the same question." He patted the seat next to him.

"Can't sleep. Too much on my mind tonight." I sat down next to him, scooting against him when he lifted his arm to snuggle. "I need to decide if I'm going to quit my job."

"Hmm. Tough decision." He didn't look away from the television, which had some ridiculous late-night cartoon on. "Would it be a bad thing if you quit?"

"I like what I do." I put my head on his shoulder. "I just don't see how I'm going to lead a pack that was just thrust back together after decades of hostility and be able to focus on a full-time job."

Silas's fingers traveled up and down my bare arm. "You can probably do more good by starting some kind of foundation with Cole's money."

"I can't ask him for money."

"Sure you can. I already asked him if he'd foot the bill for adding a workshop. He's our sugar daddy now." I turned my head to look at him, and he couldn't keep the grin from spreading across his face.

I shoved away from him with a laugh and moved to get up. I'd come downstairs for a late-night snack, not to watch television. Silas caught my hand and pulled me to straddle his lap.

"Where do you think you're going, bunny?" He moved the hair off my shoulder and ran his fingers along the strap of my top.

"I thought a snack and warm glass of milk might help me fall asleep." I shut my eyes and made a sound of approval as his hand moved across my cleavage.

"There are other things that might help you fall asleep." His lips brushed across my neck and kissed down to my breasts. "Tell me you want this too."

"I do," I breathed, already feeling like putty in his hands.

He pushed my top down under my breasts and took a nipple in his mouth, a growl vibrating against the peaked point. My hands went to his hair, digging in and encouraging him to give me more.

His erection was pressed against my pajama bottoms and I moved against him, already feeling the wetness soaking through my panties. All it had taken was his fingers against my skin to make me ready for him.

After he took my other nipple in his mouth, I pulled away, standing and staring down at him. His eyes were half closed and his boxers very obviously tented. Wasting no time, I took off my clothes, standing bare in front of him as his eyes perused my body.

He'd of course seen me naked plenty, but not like this. Not for his eyes only.

"I take back your nickname... you're a fucking vixen." He rubbed his hand down his face and chest until he got to his dick. "Fucking beautiful."

I cringed. "I prefer bunny over vixen."

He shimmied out of his boxers and kicked them to the side. "Come here."

"You think you're the boss of me?" I raised an

eyebrow and stifled my squeal when he grabbed me around the waist and pulled me onto him.

Our lips met in a feverish kiss that made me dizzy with need. His cock was pressed right up against my entrance, teasing me with the promise of what was to come.

His touches were tender and left my legs shaking and my pussy clenching at what was missing from inside.

"Silas. I need you." I buried my face in his hair, breathing in his scent.

Lifting myself slightly, I wrapped my fingers around him and lowered myself until he was fully sheathed inside me. Both of us were shaking from the intimate connection, and I stayed still, enjoying the press of my breasts against his chest and the warmth of his breath against my neck.

"Did you fall asleep?" he whispered.

Laughing, I lifted my head from his neck so I could see his sparkling eyes. "Just adjusting and savoring the feeling of you inside me."

"Mm..." He leaned back and rolled his hips. "Ride me."

I didn't argue, leaning forward and grabbing onto the back of the couch. I slid up and down his length, grinding my clit against his pelvis with every downward stroke. It wasn't long until my lower back tickled with sweat and my breaths became labored.

Silas buried his face against my chest, his short beard prickling my skin. The sounds of our bodies coming together and the feel of him against me brought me closer and closer to the edge. I couldn't move myself fast enough and chased my orgasm.

"Fuck, bunny." He smacked my ass, and I clenched around him as the skin heated.

"Do it again." I could barely speak as I rode him like I was on the final stretch of the track at the Kentucky Derby.

He spanked me harder, the sound loud in the quiet of night. My orgasm rolled through me, and my movement became erratic as my muscles tightened and pleasure spread through my limbs.

A whimper escaped as Silas stood and moved me to bend over the arm of the couch. He slid back into my slick channel and buried himself to the hilt.

My fingers dug into the couch cushion as he drilled into me, holding nothing back. He was hitting all the right spots and he reached around to rub my clit.

"Oh, God, Silas." I was trying to be quiet, but it was difficult. "Don't stop."

"Need... to... see your... face," he panted.

I looked back over my shoulder, meeting his eyes. He groaned and slammed into me one last time, filling me with his seed.

I collapsed forward onto the couch, not caring that I was making a mess of the armrest as he slid out. My entire body was satiated, and I let out a satisfied sound.

"This would make a great painting for my workshop." Silas tapped my ass and disappeared into the kitchen.

He returned with a glass of water and a hand towel.

I let him clean me before he turned off the television and scooped me up.

"Screw the sleeping schedule. You're sleeping with me tonight." I took a sip of the water, holding the glass tight as he climbed the stairs.

"We could fit in Cole's bed," I suggested as he reached the top and paused at the landing.

He looked down the hall toward his room and then at Cole's room. "Is that what you want?"

"I want whatever you're comfortable with." I bit my inner cheek because I really wanted him to at least give sleeping in the same bed with Cole a shot.

He turned toward his room but then pivoted and marched toward Cole's. "The things I do for love."

Love? A word had never felt so right.

CHAPTER TWENTY-TWO

Xander

Things had calmed down substantially in the last few weeks. For the first time in a long time, I felt like I could breathe again. I'd started seeing a therapist that was in the pack and she'd help me immensely with techniques to use when I felt like I was losing myself to my wolf.

We weren't completely sure I'd even really smelled anyone from where I was held. I was doubting it too. The SUV that had been supposedly following us could have just been a fluke.

Ivy had quit her job the week before, deciding to embrace her place as alpha of the Arbor Pack. There was no more east and west, and at first, some members had pushed back, but Ivy held her ground and told them they could leave if they weren't happy.

No one left.

"Are you ready to go?" Ivy came down the stairs, looking like something out of a dream.

She had changed over the past two weeks. An air of power swirled wherever she went, and everyone was taking notice. Including my dick.

"Yup." I finished rolling the sleeves of my flannel and followed her out to the garage. "I can't wait to see your house."

She laughed as we got into her car. "Why? It's not even going to be mine soon."

We were on our way to meet the realtor so Ivy could sign paperwork to put her house up for sale. Last week they'd packed the rest of her belongings and moved her out.

"Still, you made it your home." I wished I could show her my previous home, but I wasn't sure I could ever go back there. "Eli mentioned you four had a little fun without me, and now I feel it's only fair I get to leave my mark on the place."

She backed out of the garage and glanced over at me with a smirk. "Is that why you volunteered to come with me?"

"Damn right." I buckled my seatbelt and adjusted the volume of the radio. "And I really wanted to get out of here."

She sighed. "I don't blame you. I wished I had time to have a normal job away from here, but it's just not in the cards anymore."

"You can at least still do your research." I put my

hand over hers on the gear stick. "You're doing a great job so far."

She snorted as we pulled out onto the highway and headed toward Arbor Falls. "Only because Cole and Silas are essentially still alphas. They certainly act like it."

"It will just take time… or this is the way it's supposed to be. We still have no clue what you said to us."

The words she had said were in a language I'd never heard before. It sounded like Latin, but I didn't exactly know Latin. We'd tried remembering some words to search on the internet but had turned up nothing. Whatever it was, was something special. I felt it in my soul.

One of my favorite songs, *Lost It All* by Black Veil Brides, came on, and I turned up the volume to sing along.

Ivy said something, and I turned the music down a bit. "What?"

"I said, it's nice seeing you like this. I'm glad the therapist is helping." She smiled as she took the exit to her house. "You have an amazing voice."

"Thanks." If it wasn't for the whole wolf thing, I'd have pursued a music career, but that draws too much attention. "This is your house?"

We pulled into the driveway of a family-style craftsman, and I looked at her in surprise. Did owning a family home mean she wanted pups?

"Yup. Fell in love with it." She parked and unhooked

her seatbelt, glancing up at me. "Why are you looking at me like that?"

"Do you want pups?" When she raised her eyebrow in question, I laughed. "Babies. Do you want babies?"

"Haven't given much thought to it honestly. I've been so focused on school and then my career that I hadn't really thought of a timeline. It wasn't like there was a person who made my ovaries weep." She turned off the car and opened her door. "But maybe down the road. Far down the road."

I followed her into the house and breathed in her scent. I could smell the others' too, but hers was overwhelming. She'd made this house her safe place, and now she was letting it go.

"You could keep it." I ran my hand over the original wood on a column.

"Keep what?" She walked over to the couch and sat down. She'd left some furniture for staging since she didn't need it anymore.

"The house. Whenever we need some alone time with you, it can be our little getaway." I sat next to her and pulled her against me so her back was resting against my chest. "It can be our fuck pad."

She laughed. "We'd have to drive all the way here. I'm still not opposed to using my alpha mojo to get my way about a new treehouse being built."

"I don't think you need to use your alpha anything to get what you want." I kissed the shell of her ear. "What should we do while we wait for the realtor?"

"Hmm… I could think of a few things…" She turned

to face me, and I was about to kiss her when her phone rang. "Damn it."

She pulled it out of her purse. "Cole?... No, we're at my house to meet with the realtor, I told you that earlier." She stood and looked down at me, color draining from her face. "What?"

"What is it?" I stood, ready to take the phone from her because she looked like she was about to drop it.

"There's a fire." She handed me the phone.

My stomach turned. "How bad is it?"

"Any kind of fire isn't good. It started from the treehouse, which makes no fucking sense!" He sounded like he was in a truck. "I'm headed to get the helicopter. Silas and Eli are evacuating the pack in the surrounding area."

"What do you need me to do?" I tried to practice the breathing technique I'd been working on. It helped. Barely.

"Stay where you are. We'll come there as soon as we can. Hopefully, we can get it contained." He hung up, and I stared down at the phone in disbelief.

"Hey, stay with me." Ivy took the phone and slid it into her back pocket. "We should go help."

"We can't help with a fire." I pulled her into a hug. "It'll be fine."

We stood in the middle of her living room, holding each other. There was a little comfort in knowing the pack had a fire station and the area had just had a really wet winter. Those things worked in our favor.

"Geez, my back has been itching today." I stepped

away from Ivy and reached for the spot on my back I couldn't quite reach. I moved over to the corner of the wall and rubbed against it.

"Maybe it's your shirt label." Ivy grabbed my arm and made me turn around. She snaked her hand under the back. "Right here?"

"Yes." I nearly hissed the word as her nails scraped over the spot that had eluded me.

"Did something bite you?" She ran a thumb over a spot, pressing it and causing me to gasp as it stung. "It feels like-"

There was a knock at the door, and she stepped away. "Finally. I don't think it's a good sign that the realtor is ten minutes late, but she's supposed to be the best there is."

She went to the door to open it, leaving me trying to still scratch the spot. Maybe there was a spoon I could use.

The door squeaked slightly as it opened, and then their scent hit me.

Them.

But it wasn't just their scent, but the faint scent of kerosene that made my wolf go nuts. My ears rang and my vision tunneled as I turned to find my mate... my Ivy being held with a gun to her head.

"Hello, sixty-four. It's time for you to come home."

No.

To be continued...

Printed in Great Britain
by Amazon